# THE ITALIAN'S
# FORCED BRIDE

# THE ITALIAN'S FORCED BRIDE

BY

KATE WALKER

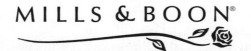

First published in Great Britain 2006
Large Print edition 2006
Harlequin Mills & Boon Limited,
Eton House, 18-24 Paradise Road,
Richmond, Surrey TW9 1SR

© Kate Walker 2006

ISBN-13: 978 0 263 18992 6
ISBN-10:      0 263 18992 9

Set in Times Roman 16½ on 19 pt.
16-0806-54066

Printed and bound in Great Britain
by Antony Rowe Ltd, Chippenham, Wiltshire

# CHAPTER ONE

ALICE HOWARD knew just who was at the door from the very first second she heard the bell ring.

She knew who it was; knew who was there. And she also knew that he was the last person on earth that she wanted to face. Even though, at the same time, he was the person she most wanted to see in all the world.

Just the thought of opening the door to him turned her legs to water so that she couldn't stand up or go to the window to look out and see if she was right about the identity of her unexpected visitor. But then she didn't need to. She was sure in her mind of that—and more so in her heart, where it mattered most.

The timing was right—just three days after she had sent the letter to tell him she had something important they had to talk about… Her hand slid down and curved protectively over the spot where she had only recently learned that her baby—and this man's child—was beginning to grow. *Something very, very important,* she had said—and it was certainly that.

The atmosphere was right too. The arrival totally out of the blue. No warning. Not even the sound of a car coming up the small country lane and pulling up outside her gate had alerted her to the fact that he was there.

And even the sound was just right. The hard, loud, unceasing ring of the bell, echoing through the quiet of the afternoon and the silence in the small house, was like an imperious, autocratic summons. As cold and proud and unyielding as Domenico himself.

*Domenico.*

There, now she'd let his name into her thoughts. She'd finally admitted who she was expecting her unwanted visitor to be.

The man whose arrival on her doorstep she was dreading most.

Or did she mean longing for most…?

She couldn't answer that and shook her dark head slowly, sending her long hair flying around her pale, oval-shaped face. Sharp white teeth worried at the fullness of her bottom lip and her blue eyes were clouded by the deep shadows left by long nights, lack of sleep and that extra little secret as well.

'Domenico.'

His name slipped from Alice's lips as she sat back on the small single bed in the tiny, shabbily decorated bedroom, hands clenched tightly in her lap as she fought against the craven impulse to rush to her feet, dash across the pale green carpet and peer out of the window.

Safely hidden behind the faded velvet curtains, of course.

But she didn't need to look. She already knew exactly what she would see. His image was imprinted on her mind, the strong features and powerful physique, black hair and dark gold eyes etched into her thoughts by the power of the love she had once felt for him. All the tears she had shed since their parting—and before—hadn't been enough to wipe away the memories of the man who had once meant more to her than her own life.

The man who had once held her heart in his

hands, to do with as he wished. But he had been totally careless of the gift she had given him. He had treated it callously and cruelly, without a thought for the way she had made herself so vulnerable to him. And so, in the end, unable to take any more, she had had to leave.

She had thought that she had gone far enough away. That by heading back to England, to her home, to the village so many hundreds of miles away from the sophisticated Italian city of Florence where he lived, she had escaped his malign influence. That here, in the quiet of the countryside, she would have a chance to lick her wounds in private and somehow find the strength to face the world again, start over.

'Alice!'

If she had had the slightest belief that she was wrong and that the person at the door was not who she feared, then that belief was shattered instantly at the sound of her name.

'Alice!'

Only Domenico used her name in that way. Only he could take the simple syllables and, with the help of his musical Italian accent lengthening the *i* in the middle to a long, soft *ee*, turn them into something so lyrical that it sounded like a poem instead of just a name.

'*Alice!*'

But there was nothing musical or poetic about the way he used her name right now.

His tone was the opposite of soft, the cold, slashing sound of his voice like a shower of sleet falling on the soft spring air, the barely controlled anger giving it a brutal edge.

'Open this door, damn you! I know you're there!'

He couldn't *know* that, Alice told herself, struggling to still the racing thud of her heart. He was simply challenging her, being deliberately provocative—being Domenico.

Domenico, who had never, to her knowledge, ever admitted to being wrong or even unsure about anything. Domenico who knew everything, understood everything, handled everything that life ever threw at him. He must have been born with that supreme self-confidence. Lying in his cot, he must have looked out on the world with the arrogance of a tiny Roman emperor, knowing he had only to make the slightest sound and his doting attendants would rush to his side.

So now he was just frustrated at the way she hadn't jumped to answer his command, the way that everyone else in his life did. He was challenging her, wanting to push her into revealing herself.

'Go away!' She mouthed the comment in the direction of the window, secure in the fact that he couldn't see her, had no proof that she was even in the house.

She had simply to stay where she was, well back from the window, hidden by the cottage's thick stone walls, and eventually his frustration would turn to boredom, boredom to anger, and he would slam himself into his car in disgust, drive away with a screech of tyres on the pebbled drive.

And she would be free of him.

For a while at least.

Oh, she knew she couldn't hope that he would get so annoyed he would leave for good—never coming back. That was too much to dream of. Domenico Parrisi didn't give up that easily. Not after just one attempt.

In fact, Domenico Parrisi didn't give up *at all*. He was renowned for it; his reputation for determination and refusal to surrender second to none.

He would be back, sooner rather than later. To

have the talk she'd said she wanted. But at least she would have had a little more breathing space. A little more time to think, and to work out just how she was going to handle things. What she was going to say to him.

It had gone suspiciously quiet outside. The awful noise of the bell ringing on and on and on had stopped, and so had the sound of Domenico's voice. She hadn't heard the car leave—but then she hadn't heard it arrive either!

Had he gone? Had she actually been lucky this time and got away with avoiding the confrontation he'd evidently planned? She couldn't quite believe it.

Edging closer to the window, she tried to peer out but the faded green velvet curtain blocked her view. Twitching it aside by just an inch or two, she leaned forward, looked out…

And looked straight into a darkly handsome face, her startled blue eyes clashing with the burning bronze gaze of the man below.

He had moved back from the cottage door and was leaning against the bonnet of the car—something sleekly low-slung and metallic grey—his long legs crossed at the ankles, strong arms folded firmly across his broad chest. The weak spring sunlight made his jet-black hair gleam and a soft breeze lifted and ruffled the shining strands. His head was thrown back, the fierce profile in stark relief against the pale blue sky.

He was waiting and watching, like some big, powerful black cat sitting patiently by the hole in the skirting board, knowing exactly where the small, nervous mouse had disappeared. And knowing just where it ultimately would have to come out of hiding and into the open again. So he was quite content to wait and watch—and pounce if his victim so much as showed a whisker.

And he was looking straight at her. Eyes hooded, mouth—a mouth that was normally a sultry, sexual temptation—drawn into a thin, controlled line, lips compressed. The coldness in his eyes seemed to slice into her like an icy laser, cutting straight through to her heart.

And then he lifted his arm, waved a hand in an imperious gesture, pointed.

The message behind that particular signal couldn't have been clearer if he'd written it in large red letters along the length of his expensive car.

Get yourself down here, it said. And be quick about it.

Immediately her mood changed.

'All right,' she muttered to him from the security of behind the pane of glass. 'All right, I'll come down. But, I warn you, you might just regret it when I do.'

So she *was* at home, Domenico reflected grimly, watching Alice's face disappear from the window. And a damn good thing that she was. Otherwise he would have made this journey for nothing. And he didn't have the time or inclination to waste precious hours on 'nothing'.

When the detective he had hired to find Alice for him had come back with this address, he'd thought long and hard about whether it was worth making the journey all this way to seek her out.

Wouldn't it have been better to dismiss her from his thoughts just as easily as Alice had been able to dismiss the months they had spent together from hers? But the problem was that once he'd let a single thought into his head, it had been followed by others, dozens of them.

Thoughts he'd told himself he'd forgotten. Memories he didn't want to recall.

Memories he damn well wasn't going to recall now!

He and Alice Howard had had a relationship. Well, he'd thought it was a relationship; she, evidently, had thought otherwise. She had just been 'having fun', she'd told him in that last cold-blooded confrontation, but now it wasn't fun any more and she was leaving.

And that was that. She had packed her bags and walked.

Walked out of his home, out of his life, out of his world. She hadn't spared a backward glance; hadn't given him any sort of explanation—just gone, making it plain that she no longer had any time for him or interest in him.

Certainly the woman who had peered down at him from the first-floor window of this tiny, shabby cottage didn't appear at all enthusiastic at seeing him. In fact, everything about her gave the opposite impression. She was staring at him as if he was some particularly nasty form of life that had just crawled out of the overgrown pond in the middle of the unkempt lawn, and she appeared to have frozen into immobility, rather than making any move to let him in.

But she had walked out on him—and that was something he wasn't used to. Truth to tell, he was always—*always*—the one who did the walking. And that was the way he liked it. It meant that when it was over, it was over. There were no hanging, frayed loose ends.

Loose ends got in the way. They could trip you up, stop you from moving on. Domenico preferred things clear-cut. Things with Alice had been far from clear-cut.

And so he had snatched at time he didn't actually have to make the journey here. He was not going to be pleased if she stayed hidden away and didn't let him in, and the whole journey was a waste of time. He certainly didn't plan on coming back again if she changed her mind a second time and decided she *did* want to see him after all.

In fact, he wasn't at all sure just why he was here now. He…

His thoughts stopped dead at the sound of the door handle moving. The white-painted wood swung open and Alice stood in the space of the doorway.

*'Dannazione!'*

Domenico swore under his breath as he felt the effect that her appearance alone had on him. The kick of response low down in his body told him the unwelcome truth about why he had been so reluctant—and yet so determined—to come here today.

He still wanted this woman.

He'd wanted her from the moment he'd first set eyes on her, and he still did, damn it! And he sure as hell didn't want to feel that way.

She was far more casually dressed than he had seen her for a long time. The loose lilac T-shirt was long, almost like a tunic over the top of black jeans, and she had pulled on a black cotton cardigan over the top, leaving it hanging open. The worn denim shaped the long, slender lines of her legs and the way the soft cotton of the T-shirt clung to the rounded curves of her hips made his mouth dry in the heat of sudden desire. Her feet were bare and looking down at the way that the small pink toes curled and flexed on the cool stone of the doorstep brought a sudden, blazing memory of how it had felt to have one of those narrow, soft feet slide erotically up and down the exposed skin of his own calf, over his knee…along his thigh…

'Well?' Alice said sharply.

The cold, brittle tone of the single word shattered the heated illusion that had gripped him. This was the woman who had walked out on him, he reminded himself. The woman who had done what no other woman had ever done.

'*Buon giorno, Signorina Howard.*'

Domenico forced himself to speak, fighting against the husky sound that the dryness in his throat had created.

Perhaps it was the sombre colour against her skin, or the way that her dark hair tumbled rather wildly about her shoulders, but she looked paler than usual, the deep blue eyes like clouded pools above the slanting cheekbones. And there was a coldness in those stunning eyes that might have frozen a lesser man, leaving him incapable of speech.

But *frozen* was not how Domenico felt. Quite the opposite. She could never look anything but stunning, and somehow the two months' absence had increased rather than lessened the impact of her deeply sensual femininity.

He had told himself that in his memories he had exaggerated the potent appeal of her beauty, the lush curves of her body, but the instant electric sting of desire that tormented him just at seeing her revealed that unfounded confidence as the lie it was.

There was no way he was over this woman. And seeing her here, like this, had driven that point home with a force that made his head spin. Everything that was male in him responded to her femaleness on the most primitive, basic level, heating his blood and demanding satisfaction right here, right now. The impulse to march across the few metres of pebbled drive between them, snatch her up into his arms and carry her inside to the nearest bed—the nearest floor— was such a struggle to resist that the tension tightened his muscles, tied painful knots in his nerves as he fought to control it.

'I understand that you wanted to talk to me,' he continued.

It seemed that the strain had reached his vocal cords too, making his voice sound harsh and raw, almost brutally aggressive. But then that only matched the cold welcome she had given him.

And she showed no sign of being pleased, or even relieved to see him. Instead, those deep blue eyes were as cold and distant as the ocean—the *English* sea, he amended, recalling the way that the water on the coast here had been so very different from the warm blue of the Mediterranean that surrounded his own country.

'So talk,' he growled in irritation.

*Talk!*

The word—the command, for that was what it was—reverberated inside Alice's head.

*Talk*, he said, standing there, lean hips propped against the low bonnet of his car, powerful arms folded across his chest like a determined barrier, beautiful eyes gleaming bronze in the weak April sunlight.

Talk.

But what could she say? What was it safe to talk about? She couldn't just plunge straight in and announce starkly that she was pregnant.

'I think we'd do better to discuss this inside.'

'If you prefer.'

His voice was hard and unyielding, totally uncompromising, just like his expression.

*This far and no further,* was what the look he shot her said. *You can bring me to your door, but you can't make me do anything I don't want to do.* And Alice felt the force of that look almost as if it had been a deliberate slap in the face.

How could she talk to a man who was so obviously armoured against her? A man who, it seemed, had dropped even the pretence of caring that he had displayed when they had been together.

But, of course, the truth was that now she knew it had only been a pretence. Then, she had been totally convinced of his honesty, and had gullibly swallowed the stories he'd spun her.

She certainly couldn't tell him just like that— totally cold. Not with her secret gnawing at her deep inside, the dread of seeing his expression when she spoke. Not knowing at all just how he would take the news of her pregnancy, this man who had openly declared that he 'didn't do marriage'. If nothing else, she needed a few moments to gather herself.

'Well, I need a drink.'

She tried to make it sound as if she didn't give a damn what *he* wanted. In fact, she was actually turning her back on him as she spoke.

'You can come in or wait out here as you please.'

She left the door open behind her as she walked back into the house, not daring even to glance back over her shoulder to see if he followed her. She didn't care if he did or not, she told herself, trying to make herself believe it. But all the while she knew that she was only kidding herself.

Just seeing him here like this had rocked her world. Already her heart was beating hard and fast inside her chest, making her breathing painfully shallow and rapid so that her head swam uncomfortably. She was shivering faintly as if she was in a state of shock, and her stomach clenched on an uncomfortable wave of nausea.

She had had to fight so hard to get away from him. And the worst battle had been with herself. But now it seemed that she had been flung back right into the maelstrom of feelings that simply being with Domenico could create; and she didn't know how to handle them.

Why was he here? Why had he finally decided, after eight long weeks, to come after her?

'One drink, then.'

She hadn't heard him come in after her, so that now his voice, sounding so suddenly behind her back, made her jump like a frightened cat, the glass she had picked up to fill with water clattering sharply against the tap.

'My, you are jumpy, aren't you?' Domenico drawled cynically. 'What's the problem? A guilty conscience?'

'Not at all.'

Alice fought for control over her voice and her hands before she put the glass under the tap to fill. But even then she had to concentrate fiercely on holding it straight and not letting the betraying tremble in her fingers give her away too much.

Somehow she managed to complete the action, turning with what she hoped was the right amount of nonchalance and taking a careful sip of her drink as she faced him again.

'It's just that I thought you were determined to stay outside. But now that you are here, what can I get you? Tea? Coffee?'

'You know that I never drink tea,' Domenico returned with a faint shudder. He had never understood her very English addiction to the drink and always tried to avoid so much as a sip of it when she made a pot for herself. 'Surely you can't have forgotten that already?'

'Out of sight, out of mind.'

Oh, he hadn't liked that! The burning glare he turned on her made her throat constrict so that she thought she would choke on her second sip of water.

But angering him was a bad mistake. She was going to need him in a mood to listen and if she drove him into one of his black rages then there was little chance of that ever happening. So she carefully toned down the sharpness of her response.

'For all I know, you might have had a complete change of heart about a lot of things in the time since we were together,' Alice went on with careful coolness. 'And I'm not at all sure that I really knew you that well anyway.'

'We spent over six months together.'

'Six months in which you were at work or in some other country for more time than you were ever in Italy,' she reminded him.

'I warned you what it would be like,' Domenico stated flatly. 'I never left you with any illusion that it could be otherwise.'

'No,' Alice admitted. 'You were perfectly straight about that.'

He had been totally upfront about the fact that his work was his life. He hadn't made it to where he was—from nowhere to head of the multi-million-pound Parrisi computer empire—by sitting back and contemplating. Domenico was a force to be reckoned with.

No one knew very much about him. He kept his background—where he came from, who he was—intensely private. It was rumoured that he never slept, rarely ate. That the only leisure activity he had time for were the nights he spent with beautiful women.

The beautiful, glamorous women who were seen on his arm at all the right places.

But, as she had cause to know only too well, it was not the women who were seen on his arm that mattered.

'So that wasn't why you walked out?'

The question took her by surprise. As did the fact that he suddenly seemed so very much closer. Dangerously so.

When had he moved? He must have been as silent on his feet as a panther stalking its prey, prowling up behind her when she wasn't looking and making the small kitchen seem suddenly even smaller until no matter which way she turned the place was full of Domenico. His height and strength dominated the space between them, the sheer impact of his tautly muscled body overwhelming. He had tugged his tie loose at the neck and unfastened the top two buttons and she could see the faint shadowing of dark body hair in the opening of the light blue cotton. The clean, masculine scent of his skin, overlaid with the subtle tang of some expensive cologne, filled her nostrils and the soft sound of his breathing was in her ears.

Her heart had started to thud again, but this time it was with a very different sort of pulse, one that unwillingly she had to acknowledge that she recognised only too well. This was the heavy, heated beat of awareness that had always assailed her in the past. The way that she had felt from the first moment she had seen him and had never really recovered from since.

It was the sheer concentrated physical impact that he had on her. And the pulse that throbbed through her veins was one of deep, sensual arousal. It was as if everything that was male in him was calling to her own essential femininity on the deepest, most primitive level, in a way that made her head spin.

'I told you why I left.'

'Yeah, you stopped having fun.'

There was something in his voice that caught and held her. Some soft undertone that seemed to reach out and enclose her, like the delicate but constricting lines of a spider's web. She felt it coil round her, lightly seductive but dangerously transfixing.

'Why was that, *cara*, hmm?'

'I…'

Her voice had failed her, no matter how hard she tried to make it work. Her mouth opened and closed but no sound came out. She felt she must look like some stupid, gaping fish, but something about her expression made Domenico smile.

'When did the fun go out of things? Because it never did for me.'

'Never?'

Was that stupid, squeaky little voice really hers?

'Never.' Domenico's echoing of the word was much lower, deeper, rich with a sensuality that tugged at something deep inside her.

'Coffee.' She tried for common sense, for practicality.

Domenico shook his dark head slowly, that smile growing wickedly.

'I think not,' he murmured.

No? Once again Alice tried to form the word but failed, her throat closing. Nervously she slicked her tongue over painfully dry lips, determined to try again, only to have the determination evaporate like mist before the sun as she saw the way his bronze gaze dropped to follow the betraying movement, the intensity with which it fixed on her mouth.

'What?' she managed to croak, rough and uneven.

'There is something I would like so much more.'

And before she could snatch in another breath his mouth came down on hers, taking it in a slow, seductive kiss.

# CHAPTER TWO

HE HADN'T been able to resist it, Domenico admitted to himself. He had come into the house determined to hold back, to keep himself to himself, to watch and wait, and only decide what his next move should be when he had found out just which way the land was lying.

But from the moment he'd set eyes on Alice once again, he had been caught up in the familiar burn of desire that always took his body by storm whenever she was around.

He had been determined to stay outside at first. At least that way he could keep some distance between himself and the beguiling enticement offered by her sexy body. An enticement that twisted in his guts, coiled around his senses, stopped him from thinking straight.

He wasn't going to jump in with both feet this time, he'd told himself. Not the way he had done last time. Then he had wanted her in his life just five minutes after meeting her, had had her in his bed within a day. He had been so obsessed, so physically enslaved by her that he hadn't been able to *think*, except with one very basic part of his anatomy.

And look where that had got him! After six short months she had walked out on him, declaring she'd had enough and she wasn't coming back.

So this time he had vowed that he was going to take things steady.

That he was going to think before he acted, pause before he moved. And was very definitely going to put his brain in charge instead of his libido.

But from the moment she had appeared in the doorway he had known that thinking was not what he wanted to be doing. He had fought down the carnal urges that stung at him, not even allowing himself to look too closely at her—until she had turned to walk away.

The sway of her hips had been his downfall. The sight of the neat, curved behind in the tight black jeans had set his pulse rate soaring, scrambling his thought processes.

He had been without this woman in his bed for two months and that was long enough.

More than long enough.

And he was going to do something about it.

'Something I want a hell of a lot more,' he murmured now against her mouth, 'than any damn coffee.'

Her first response was to stiffen under his caress. To freeze into immobility, her slender body held taut, inches away from his.

But she hadn't pulled away. She wasn't fighting him.

So he kissed her again. Harder this time. Firmer.

He slid his hands up into the dark silkiness of her hair, cupping the fine bones of her skull in his palms as he angled her head so that it was positioned just right.

And she went with him all the way. Let him do just as he pleased. Her eyes were closed and there was a new and very different tension in her muscles now. Her mouth softened under his, her lips parting on a sigh of response, of surrender, but she hadn't yet let herself go, hadn't leaned into him.

'Alice, *carina*…'

He pressed home his advantage, sliding one

hand down the long length of her spine, curving it around her waist and sliding it under the loose-fitting T-shirt, bringing it up to cup the warm, soft side of one breast.

She jumped slightly, tensed a little, then stilled. But her clinging mouth never left his; her tongue danced with his in an echo of the intimacy she was inviting.

But that tiny hesitation warned him not to rush things. To slow down, take a step back. If he pushed too hard now he might drive her away and that was not what he wanted at all.

And so he eased his mouth away from hers, brought his hand back down to her waist, smoothing the lilac cotton straight as he did so.

'No...' he said slowly, softly, the effort it cost him to keep it that way, the stinging protest from his heavily aroused body, putting a convincing unevenness into his tone. 'No.'

And watched her eyes fly open in disconcerted amazement.

'No?' she asked sharply, obviously bewildered.

Just what was happening? Alice asked herself, struggling to get a grip on her feelings—and on Domenico's constantly changing moods.

He had arrived here in a state of cold anger, obviously totally armoured against her, so much so that she had been convinced he wouldn't even set foot in the house. He had insisted that she talk and made her afraid that he knew her secret. Then suddenly he had changed again, become Domenico the seductive—a Domenico she knew only too well.

Perhaps it was because she knew that Domenico so well that she had responded to him so easily, let her defences down without thinking. One touch of his lips on hers and she had been lost. Lost in the so-familiar taste, the familiar scent, the heat of his skin, the strength of his hands on her head.

Lost in the sensual spell that he wove so effortlessly.

'Not a wise move,' Domenico said now. 'At least, not yet.'

The audacious assumption of that 'not yet' took her breath away. She had to clamp her mouth tight shut, teeth digging into her tongue, so as not to fling a furious retort at him, her fingers itching to swipe the self-assured smile from his stunning face.

She knew she had only herself to blame for that arrogant confidence. After all, he had only to touch her and she became putty in his hands. It was as if they had never been apart. He knew just the way to hold her, to kiss her, to caress her, and she went up in flames. Her body was still shaking from the erotic assault of his kiss. That brief, fleeting touch of his hard fingers against her breast, so newly sensitised by the changes in her body, had set her senses singing.

The need for more was a deep ache low down in her body, a heated pulse between her legs. But the emotional need was worse; the knowledge of what she had wanted so much from this man and how he had broken her heart when she had realised that he would never provide it.

'Coffee,' she said again, hoping she sounded more determined than she felt.

'Coffee,' Domenico echoed, but he didn't move away. He didn't smile, either, but watched her, his burning gaze disturbingly intent. She felt like a small, uncertain creature being watched by a large, predatory jungle cat, one that was trying to make up his mind whether it was worth the trouble of pouncing.

So had that kiss meant nothing to him at all?

Had he just wanted to see how she would react? Or had he not been able to stop himself?

Or worse, had he simply kissed her because he could—as an act of power?

The thought sent a shiver down her spine, making her hand unsteady as she reached for the coffee jar and the cafetière.

Now was completely the wrong time to remember that one of the side effects of her pregnancy was the fact that she had suddenly developed a hatred for the scent of coffee grounds. The smell caught in her throat, twisted round her stomach, making her feel horribly nauseous and unwell.

Briefly she closed her eyes, fighting the sensation.

'Is something wrong?' Domenico had noticed her reaction and pounced swiftly.

'No!'

Alice forced her eyes open sharply, fighting to hold her breath, not to inhale the nauseating smell as she spooned coffee into the glass jug.

'I'm fine.'

'You don't look it.'

'I—I wasn't expecting you to just turn up like that.'

If she was honest, she hadn't expected him to come here at all. The most she had hoped for was a phone call in response to her note saying that they needed to talk. The way he had appeared on her doorstep had rocked her right off balance.

'I couldn't stay away.'

'And you expect me to believe that?'

Broad shoulders lifted in a shrug that said he didn't really give a damn whether she did or not.

'You're not an easy woman to find.'

'Maybe I didn't want to be found.'

But then the realisation of just what he had said hit her hard, bringing her head up sharply.

'You were looking for me?'

Her voice squeaked ridiculously as her eyes flew to his face. It was difficult to read anything into that dark, shuttered expression, the way his eyes met hers head on, unyielding and unrevealing.

'Of course.'

'I find that hard to believe.'

She hoped she sounded calmer than she felt,

but the tremor in her hands scattered the coffee over the edge of the jug and onto the worktop.

'Damn!'

Painfully aware of Domenico's dark bronze eyes on her pink face, she snatched up a piece of paper towel and swiped at the spilled coffee grounds, only succeeding in sending them flying further.

'Let me.'

She jumped sharply as Domenico's hand came down over her own, stilling the nervous movement. In a moment, the mess had been cleared up, swiftly and efficiently and using only one hand. And what made her tremble inside was the way that the other hand still lingered on hers, its hold so light but somehow impossible to break away from.

'I'm all fingers and thumbs!' she managed, her voice shaking with nervous response. Her heart was racing, thudding against the wall of her chest, making her breathless and unsteady.

That burning gaze dropped to their joined hands.

'But beautiful,' he said, so softly, and his accent was so thick on the two words that for a second she blinked uncertainly, wondering if she had heard right.

'What?'

'You have beautiful hands…'

Domenico's thumb moved as he spoke, stroking down the length of her middle finger, over the knuckle and smoothing the skin of her hand. His touch was warm and delicate and made her bare toes curl on the terracotta tiles of the kitchen floor, a sensual shiver snaking its way down her spine.

'*Bella.*'

'Dom…' Alice tried, the word drying on her lips. And it was only as the silence closed in around them that she realised that, unable to finish, she had croaked the shortened form of his name that she had used when they were together.

The shortened, *affectionate* form of his name.

The one that it had taken her so long to work round to using.

The one that, she had once thought, he had allowed only her to use. She had been so proud of that small fact, thinking that it meant she was somehow special to him.

'Why would I not want to find you when you are so beautiful? I said, you have beautiful hands…'

Once more that caressing thumb moved over Alice's skin, making her shudder in response.

'And a beautiful face.'

That burning gaze lifted to lock with hers, holding her transfixed and unable to look away. The touch that held her fingers still kept them captive while his other hand rose, touched her forehead, her temple, traced a heated path down the side of her cheek, coming to rest underneath her jaw line, lightly cupping her chin. The way he held her lifted her face towards his, forcing her to look into the heated depths of his eyes.

And what she saw there was something she recognised only too well.

Desire.

Stark, burning, undisguised desire.

A physical need that turned his gaze molten, that made his pupils expand, turn jet black, deep and impenetrable.

A desire that she knew was burning in her own veins, woken by the touch of his hands on her skin, the scent of his body all around her.

'Dom…' She tried again but he wasn't listening.

'You have beautiful eyes,' he murmured, leaning forward to drop a warm kiss on one eyelid, pressing it closed. 'And beautiful hair.'

Behind the enclosing darkness of her lids, she felt his mouth on her hair, felt another kiss whisper across the silky strands, and knew the sudden clutch of a harsh, primitive hunger low down in her body, pulsing cruelly.

Too cruelly, too heavily to let her think straight.

'And a very, very beautiful mouth.'

Even though her eyes were still closed she knew that he was very near. She could feel the warmth of his breath on her lips, almost taste it in her mouth.

He was going to kiss her again, she knew. And if he did then she would be lost. Helpless. Unable to resist him.

She had barely escaped with her sanity a moment ago when he had taken her into his arms. She had almost surrendered totally to him then, giving in to feelings she couldn't control.

No!

From behind the protective cover of her eyelids, she mentally shook herself fiercely.

She was not going to let this happen to her. Not going to give in to those feelings. They were not stronger than her, not uncontrollable. They were habit; nothing more!

She had been with Domenico for six months. They had been lovers from the start; she hadn't been able to resist him. And in that time she had grown so strongly accustomed to his kisses, his caresses. He knew just where to touch—how to kiss. And her body, so well attuned to his, responded instinctively, like the finest of musical instruments to the touch of a master.

It was only habit, she told herself. It sounded right—so why didn't it help?

'Alice…' Domenico breathed and she forced her eyes open, finding that he was even closer than she had thought. His face was only inches from her own, with his eyes burning into hers, the impossibly long, rich black lashes almost brushing her skin when he blinked.

And she couldn't look away, even when he moved just that last tiny bit closer and let his mouth brush hers. Just a touch. The briefest, lightest touch before he lifted his head away again. But just a touch was all it took to set her body clamouring again.

'Dom, please,' she sighed. 'Don't…stop…'

She felt that sinfully beautiful mouth smile against her own, and knew with a terrible sinking of her heart just what was coming.

'"Don't. Stop"?' Domenico questioned silkily. 'Or…"Don't stop"?'

There was no way she could answer him. She couldn't even answer herself to explain what she had meant. Even as she'd formed the words, her mind had been warring with itself, torn between the two meanings, wanting to say them both—neither—but never, ever able to decide between the two.

Domenico wasn't waiting for an answer. Bending close again, he took her mouth with his, tilting his head just so to get the perfect angle, the exact pressure he wanted, to let his tongue slide along the barely closed line of her lips.

And Alice knew she was lost. She had been so close to insanity that first time. This time she had no hope of holding back.

This wasn't habit, or anything like it, she told herself as the hot waves of sensuality broke over her, drowning her thoughts. This was passion, carnal hunger, need—desire.

Lust.

*Love?*

Oh, dear God, no! Not love.

Please let love not be part of this. Not any more!

Lust she could cope with. Desire she understood. Passion—Domenico had always brought out a burning, searing passion in her. One she couldn't control; couldn't escape. It had been her downfall from the start—and it looked as if it was going to pull her right down that heated path again.

But she didn't want to be in love with him. That had hurt too much. So much that she had barely escaped with her sanity.

'Don't tell me to stop,' Domenico muttered against her mouth, and it was impossible to tell if it was an order or if he was pleading with her, begging her not to say it, not to hold him back.

'I—'

'I can't stop!' It was harsher, thicker, roughened by the same hunger that was firing through her veins.

Between each word he snatched another kiss, each one harder, stronger, deeper than before.

And each kiss broke down another part of Alice's resistance, chipping away at it until it crumbled under the onslaught and had her clinging to him, arms tight around his neck, soft body pressed up against his hardness, her mouth opening under his, inviting more, inviting him in.

'I can't stop! I won't!'

'Don't,' Alice choked and this time she knew exactly what she meant to say; what she wanted.

What she wanted was to know this powerful passion just once more. To feel his strength around her, his touch on her skin, his kiss on her mouth.

She might be deceiving herself but deep inside her heart there was a tiny speck of hope. A small glow that time was fanning into a flame. A flame that no common sense would ever extinguish, no matter how hard she tried.

*I couldn't stay away.*

The words swung round and round in her head, drowning out all other thoughts.

*You're not an easy woman to find.*

He had been looking for her. He hadn't just arrived here because of the letter she had sent him. He had been looking for her. And now he was here, and she was in his arms, and he was kissing her.

And the powerful throb of her need for him would drive her mad if she didn't give in to it.

'Don't stop…'she sighed against his mouth and sensed rather than saw the hard, quick smile of deep satisfaction that curved those sinfully seductive lips.

'I won't,' he promised deeply. 'I swear to you I won't stop until we're both too exhausted to think—too sated to breathe.'

And, gathering her up into his arms, he turned towards the door.

'Upstairs?' he muttered, his voice dark and husky, his accent more pronounced than ever before.

'Upstairs,' Alice murmured in acceptance, knowing that this was what she wanted, no matter what happened afterwards.

# CHAPTER THREE

IF THE kitchen had seemed small with Domenico in it, then her bedroom appeared to have shrunk to doll's-house proportions. His dark strength and size dwarfed everything, standing out starkly amongst the white and green flowered decor, the elderly pine furniture.

At one side of the room the roof sloped downwards so that he had to stoop, bending low, as he carried her towards the bed. And even as he laid her on the old-fashioned quilted bedspread and came to sit beside her, he still had to keep his head bent so as not to bang it against the ceiling.

But then he had also to keep his head low to capture her mouth in another of those long, powerful, drugging kisses that shattered her thought processes, drove her senses wild and had her clasping her hands behind his neck, fingers threading through the jet-black softness of his hair, and pulling his face down towards hers, while she strained upwards to meet him.

'I've missed this... Missed it so damn much.'

It was just a rough mutter, almost incomprehensible in the thickness of Domenico's accent, blending with the harshness that desire put onto his tongue.

But Alice didn't need to hear the words clearly to understand. She could feel the strength of his need for her in the forceful touch of his hands, the impatient, urgent way he tugged the cardigan down her arms and off, pushing the loose T-shirt aside at her waist. Hard fingers burned their way across her skin, shaping the curve of her body, smoothing upwards over the lines of her ribcage.

Her breath caught in her throat as each big hand curved around the soft underside of her breasts, cupping the warm skin.

'No bra?' he questioned softly, the gleam deep in the darkness of his eyes telling her how much that small discovery pleased him.

'No—I...'

She caught in her breath at the realisation of just how close she had come to giving away her secret.

She had avoided wearing a bra whenever

possible over the past few weeks because of the way it made her feel. With her breasts newly sensitive and tender, she avoided the constriction of the underwear as much as she could, finding even the faint pressure of satin and lace almost unbearable at times.

Already she could tell that her body had altered. That her figure was developing, ripening, becoming more rounded. She was so sensitive to the changes herself but would Domenico too see the difference in the body he had once, not so long ago, known so intimately? Would he feel…?

But then those knowing hands closed over her breasts and she found that the new and heightened sensitivity to his touch made her mind swim, her head falling back against the pillows, his name escaping her on a long moan of delight.

'You like that?'

Domenico's smile had nothing in it but the deep, predatory satisfaction of a sexual male at the realisation that his touch could send a woman spinning out of control. He seemed to have taken her sudden gasp of response, her indrawn breath as nothing more than the natural reaction of uncontrolled delight he expected.

'Oh yes, you like that,' he declared with arrogant conviction. 'I *know* you like that—and that you like this.'

Slowly, deliberately, he rubbed the pads of his thumbs over her taut and yearning nipples, smiling his dark pleasure, watching her writhe as the stinging electric current of pleasure ran through her.

'You see, *I* have not forgotten! For me it is not "out of sight, out of mind"! You have never been out of my mind since that day when I came home to find you had gone.'

'Never?' Alice croaked, her mouth dry with the need that was burning her up.

'Never,' Domenico assured her. 'How could I ever think to forget this…?'

His lips took hers, the hard pressure, the intimate dance of his tongue, heightening the heated pleasure she already felt, raising it to boiling point until she felt that her brain had melted with the blaze of it.

'Or this…?'

The feel of that wicked mouth closing over her breast loosened the last remnants of any control Alice had over her tongue. The increased sensitivity that her pregnancy had brought turned his gentle suckling into a pleasure-pain that was like a wild explosion along the path of every single nerve she possessed.

'Domenico!'

His name was a moan of delight, a long, yearning sigh of need. She moved instinctively to help him ease the T-shirt from her body, lay tense with anticipation as he unfastened the black jeans and slid them down the length of her legs, tormenting every inch of her skin with hot, ruthlessly arousing kisses as he went.

'Oh, please!' Alice cried out sharply. 'Domenico—please!'

It was impossible to hold back, impossible to stem the tide of hunger that had her in its grip. She didn't know how Domenico kept his control, what ruthless grip he had on his passion so that he wasn't tearing off his own clothes, flinging himself upon her, easing the hunger of his body in the welcoming warmth of her own.

Because he *was* hungry for her. How could he not be when the forceful evidence of his body's need strained against the constriction of his trousers, crushed into the cradle of her pelvis by the weight and strength of him? The heat of it reached her through the fine material, seeming to scorch her skin and making her move restlessly under his imprisoning bulk.

The friction of her skin against his aroused body made Domenico groan aloud, flinging his proud head back, dark eyes glittering as he looked down into her upturned, rose-flushed face.

'Oh, please…' he echoed mockingly, in a mercilessly accurate mimicry of her tone.

One long-fingered hand swept down the length of her body, from the burning cheek, down over the smooth skin of her rounded shoulder, pausing for a tormenting second on the swell of her breast where the hardened nipple pushed wantonly at his palm, seeming to demand more of the electrifying pleasure he had given it only seconds before. But this time Domenico spared her only a second of the sensual delight before sliding his palm down further, lower, easing under the elastic at the top of her knickers, closing over the hot, damp curls at the juncture of her thighs.

'So what is this, hmm, Alicia, *mi bella*? Could it be that you too are remembering just what it was like? That perhaps you have not forgotten…?'

*Forgotten!* The word was like a roar of horror in her thoughts, one she had to deny.

Forgotten? How could she have forgotten anything? She had tried to forget—tried to wipe every last memory of her time with Domenico from her mind—but had failed. The endless, restless nights she had spent alone, trying to sleep, were evidence of that. The hours when she had thought of nothing but Domenico, the long, sensual hours she had spent with him in the privacy of the big, deep bed in his Milan apartment or in the villa outside Florence, the wild abandon of their lovemaking, the sensual satisfaction that had left her exhausted but contented, right to the depths of her soul.

How could she ever have forgotten that?

Even when she fell asleep her dreams were full of burning, erotic images, memories that stirred her blood and heated her body so that she tossed and turned, often moaning aloud in the night. So many times she had woken in a tangle of bedclothes, with her heart racing, her breath coming wildly, her skin sheened with the sweat that simply imagining him here with her had brought to the surface.

So now, with her dreams made reality, with Domenico's strength surrounding her, his hands caressing her body, the clean, male scent of his skin in her nostrils, she knew only too well what she had been missing; what had kept her from any real sense of rest every night they had been apart. The emptiness that only he could fill.

And she knew there was no way at all she could turn back now.

She didn't care if it was only for today, if this one last time with Domenico was all she would have, if they had any future—the future of which his appearance at the cottage seemed to hold out a promise to her. The only thing she had was here and now, and she had to grab at it with both hands because she felt that she would die if she did not.

And so she stirred once more under his imprisoning weight, deliberately arching her back slightly to press herself against the heated swell of his erection, bringing her hands up to tug at the buttons on his shirt, working them from their fastenings.

'I've not forgotten,' she admitted roughly, hiding her face against his cheek so that she didn't have to look into his eyes as she spoke, pressing her lips so close to the olive-toned skin that she felt the faint beginnings of the dark stubble against their softness. 'Never forgotten. How could I?'

Domenico's response was a laugh of triumph, low in his throat, and his hands came up to help her with the buttons, swiftly and efficiently dealing with them in contrast to the fumbling hash she had been making of it. A couple of seconds and his shirt was free. Sitting up slightly, he pushed it back, shedding both it and the superbly tailored jacket in one go, tossing them to one side without a care for the way that the beautiful garments tumbled into a crumpled heap on the floor.

But she had forgotten this, Alice admitted to herself. Well, not forgotten how beautiful his skin was, how smooth and sleek, like hot olive silk, sliding tautly over the powerful muscles, the straight, square shoulders. But in her mind she had been unable to hold on to just how sensual a delight Domenico's stunning body was, both to look at and to touch. Across his chest it was hazed with jet-black hair that she had always loved to feel underneath her fingertips, tracing the lines of it along the powerful bones of his ribcage and down, down to where the most intensely masculine part of him throbbed below the narrow waist.

When she had thought that she would never be able to do so again, having the freedom to touch him in this way was such an erotic charge that it went straight to her head like a gulp of the strongest brandy, making her giddy with pleasure and excitement in the space of a heartbeat. She couldn't hold back, had to stroke, to caress, to *feel*. She even found the nerve to press her lips against the heated flesh, remembering the unique taste of his skin, the scent of it, the sensation of feeling the strong, heavy beat of his heart beneath her mouth, the sound of it like thunder in her ears.

'Alice!' Domenico groaned in raw response, his loss of control showing in the way that the sound of her name again became not the soft English pronunciation, but the much more exotic *Aleeece*, a version that only he had ever used.

Hard hands pushed under the fall of her hair, clenching round the shining dark length and wrenching her head back as he clamped his lips down savagely on her mouth again. Still holding her prisoner with one hand, he fumbled impatiently with his belt, the fastening of his trousers, cursing in violent Italian when the clasp would not open quickly enough.

'Let me…' Alice managed, scarcely any more in control or any less clumsy as she dealt with the fastening, slid down the zip so that his erection spilled, hot and hard, into her seeking hands.

And with that one, soft touch, any remaining control that Domenico possessed evaporated right away. With her name hissing through his teeth on a sound that was somehow both violent and tender, he pushed her back down against the pillows, one hand still holding her head at just the right angle so that he could kiss her hard and strong and deeply intimately. The other hand, more roughly, pulled at the scrap of satin and lace that was all the covering she still had on. So roughly that she heard the delicate material tear, felt the elastic band at the waist split completely.

Not that she cared a damn. All she cared about was the feel of Domenico's mouth on hers, the hot thrust and flavour of his tongue invading her, tasting the essence of her. And below her waist those knowing fingers were now wreaking havoc on her most intimate senses, touching, stroking, teasing, tantalising, *exciting*, until she felt that she would explode with the force of the sensual stimulation.

But just as she felt she must abandon herself totally to the stunning sensations, the wicked provocation stopped and Domenico pushed one long, hair-roughened knee between her thighs, moving her legs apart and opening her up to him.

'This is what I remember,' he muttered, his accent so thick and pronounced that the words were all but incomprehensible. 'This is what I had with you—what I wanted from you—what I always wanted...'

Wrenching his mouth from hers, he took a couple of seconds to administer a sensual onslaught to her breasts, taking first one and then the other nipple into his mouth and suckling hard, building up a pleasure so savage it was almost a torture to endure. And before she had come down from the brainstorm of delight that he'd created, he lifted his powerful body, positioning himself exactly at the spot where she craved him most, the hot power pushing at her throbbing core.

'And I've certainly never forgotten *this*…' he muttered, thick and raw, pushing himself into her in one long, powerful thrust.

Alice was already so close to total fulfilment that just the feel of him almost took her over the edge. In less than the space of a heartbeat she was clinging to him, arching her hungry body closer and closer, opening herself to him, welcoming the force of his possession.

He thrust in as deep as he could go, withdrew, but only to push forward again, hard and strong and utterly devastating. One more pulse was all it took to splinter Alice's control into tiny pieces and have her spinning wildly and totally into a whirling vortex of delight, abandoning herself so completely that she lost all track of time and place, lost consciousness, oblivious to anything but the explosive sensations that suffused her body, and the powerful, forceful, dominant male who had made her so entirely his.

And somewhere, in the seconds before the unconsciousness of ecstasy took her over completely, she heard Domenico's hoarse, wild cry of fulfilment and knew that he too had lost himself in the blazing consummation of their lovemaking.

She had no idea how long it took her to come back down to earth. She only knew that as she floated hazily, lazily, back to reality, her body still humming with the aftershocks of the wild delight that had taken hold of her, all she could hear in her mind, in her memory were the echoes of the words Domenico had said, the things he had revealed in the heat of their passion—and before.

*I couldn't stay away.*

*You're not an easy woman to find.*

And then that final, triumphant, totally abandoned declaration: *And I've certainly never forgotten this,* as he'd taken possession of her, made her his.

She wasn't too sure just what would happen now; didn't know quite what Domenico's next move might be or how he would want to deal with things, but right now she had to admit that she didn't really care.

All that mattered was that he was here, with her, in this bed. He had been looking for her and as soon as she had written to him he had come at once, not even hesitating, not phoning or writing but appearing here, in person, declaring that he couldn't stay away. And he had just made love to her in a way that surely revealed a depth of feeling she had never suspected before.

There might be some awkwardness; they certainly had a lot of things to sort out. She needed to know the truth about Pippa Marinelli, and she had yet to tell Domenico that he was about to become a father. But all that could wait until the right moment. They had time, she was sure of that. Time to talk, to *really* talk, to put things right— and then, hopefully, move forward into a future.

But for now, Domenico was back. He was in her bed, and he had just made wonderful, stunning, mind-blowing love to her. For now that would do. All the rest would follow in its own good time.

Sated, exhausted, wonderfully content, she drifted asleep.

Consciousness returned slowly. Swimming back to the surface from the deep, deep sleep into which she had fallen, it was the silence that struck her first.

Had Domenico fallen asleep too? Was he still asleep? Still in the relaxed, totally satisfied mood into which he had collapsed with a cry of fulfilment just after her own?

Now was the time that she could tell him, she thought. Now, while he was at ease and languid with pleasure. She could tell him the reason she had asked him to come here and hope to have a fair hearing. Maybe she could even have some hope of a future for herself and her child that included the baby's father.

But as she came more awake herself, she realised that this was an unexpected, uncomfortable, strained, *watchful* sort of silence. One that tugged at her nerves, twisting some uncertain, wary, uneasy sensation deep in the pit of her stomach. She had no idea what gave her that feeling. Domenico was still lying beside her; she could feel the heat of his long body, the dip in the mattress underneath his weight. He was probably, like her, just coming back to wakefulness.

And if she knew Domenico, he would be stirring in other ways too. He had always had extraordinary powers of recovery, and a demanding sexual appetite. Glorious, explosive, orgasmic as it had been, that one passionate coming together would not be enough to satisfy him. He would already be anticipating a repeat performance, perhaps was already aroused...

But some instinct warned her that that was not the case. There was something in the atmosphere that was not the indolent, sensual, indulgent feeling she had anticipated. Some unexpected tension in the powerful masculine frame next to her, some unusual rhythm to his breathing alerted her that his mood had changed—and not in the way that she had anticipated.

It sent a cold whisper of unease sliding down her spine, chilled the passion-warmed skin, stilled her stretching limbs.

Slowly, uncertainly, she opened her eyes and looked straight up into the cold bronze stare of the man beside her.

He had woken before her, in fact. Woken first and, levering himself up into a half-upright position, had rested his elbow on the pillow, supporting his dark head on one hand, and had been watching her silently and intently as she lay asleep. Perhaps it had been some unconscious awareness of that silent scrutiny, some touch on her skin as if that stare had an actual physical force, that had penetrated the depths of exhaustion into which she had fallen and brought her slowly back to consciousness. But she had no idea why.

And that stunning, harshly carved, beautifully masculine face above her was giving nothing away. His features might have been set in stone for all the response he gave to the tentative, uncertain smile she gave, the wary attempt at a greeting. The glowing eyes were hooded, all emotion hidden from her, and the sensual, sexy mouth was set in a firm, unyielding line, no trace of an answering smile curving it up at the corners.

'Hi…' she managed softly, trying for another smile, only to have it fade away weakly in the face of his unresponsive expression. 'H-how long have you been awake?'

Domenico ignored the question, not even sparing it a second or two of consideration. Instead he looked her up and down, his eyes pure ice as they took in her relaxed body, still sprawled in the indolent aftermath of the sexual explosion that had shaken her. A slow, emotionless assessment swept over her in the long moment before the gaze returned once more to her uncertain and watchful face.

'No fun any more, huh?' he drawled, obvious disbelief in every word. 'Well, I'm sorry, Alicia, *cara*—but I really don't believe you. I think that what happened just now proved you a liar. And not a very good one, at that.'

'I—I...'

Alice struggled for words, trying to find some answer, any answer for him, but failing miserably. She knew that the hot colour she could feel rushing into her face was flooding her body too, the rosy colour betraying the way his words had caught her on the raw, leaving her unable to find anything to say.

'I think that that very definitely comes under the heading *fun*,' Domenico went on, totally ignoring her consternation, her awkward attempt to respond. 'And it was the sort of *fun* I would very much like to enjoy again—and again—until I've had my fill. Which is why I came after you, *bella mia*. You see, you may have claimed that you were growing jaded, that you were no longer getting what you wanted from our relationship, but I was most definitely *not* getting tired. I still want you—more than ever, in fact. And as long as I want you, then this relationship continues. No woman walks out on me—none ever has and none ever will.'

Leaning forward, he dropped a kiss on her

startled mouth, but it was a cold, emotionless kiss, a kiss of pure control and not of feeling. There was not even any hint of passion or desire in it. All emotion had been wiped from it, leaving it cold and indifferent, chilling her right through to her soul.

'This relationship isn't over, Alice, not until I say so. As long as I want you, you stay—and you only leave when I give you permission to go.'

# CHAPTER FOUR

ALICE felt as if that kiss had been a slap in the face.

A hard, cruel, cold-blooded slap that had knocked all the sense from her thoughts, leaving her gasping for breath like a stranded fish, her mind reeling in pain.

'I… You…'

If he had woken her by dumping a bucket full of icy water right over her head, she couldn't have been more shocked, more horrified. With a terrible sense of devastation she felt all her hopes and dreams, those lovely warm, anticipatory dreams, those promising, positive dreams, evaporate out of her heart, leaving her shivering in shock as reality hit home.

*As long as I want you, you stay.*

*That* was why Domenico had come after her. Not because he still cared about her—if in fact he had ever really cared—but because he felt he

owned her. He regarded her more as a possession, as something that was his and stayed his as
long as he wanted it to.

The thought slashed at her, stabbing straight to
her weak and foolish heart and wounding it so
badly she thought she might faint from the pain.
In an instinctive reaction of self-protection she
grabbed at the sheets, yanking them up to cover
her exposed body, needing desperately to hide at
least some part of her from those coldly assessing, coldly possessive eyes.

But somehow the gesture had exactly the
opposite effect. Eyes like bronze chips of ice
watched her frantic reaction with an almost ana-
lytical interest. Domenico was saying nothing,
his beautifully carved features expressing
nothing, but there was something in his stare, in
the set of that once sensual, now deeply controlled
mouth that said without words that he regarded
her response as foolish and totally unnecessary.
After all, he'd seen everything there was to see,
touched everything, kissed everything, so what
was the point in trying to hide now?

Because those kisses had been Judas kisses!
Alice wanted to fling at him. Because they had

been lying, deceiving gestures, seeming to speak of caring—she had even been foolish enough to allow the word *love* into her mind. And all the time he had been thinking only of power, of a ruthless need to impose his dominance over her, and to get her exactly where he wanted her—in his bed and at his mercy.

'I don't....' She tried again but her voice still wasn't ready to express how she felt. Shock seemed to have paralysed her vocal cords and as soon as she tried to speak she just managed a couple of words before the sound faded into an embarrassing and revealing squeak.

'You don't...?' Domenico questioned and his faintly mocking tone caught her on the raw, new strength flaring through her, her courage bolstered by a wave of anger.

'Don't I get any say in this matter?'

'Any say?'

Domenico appeared to consider the question, though she was quite sure that his mind was already made up. That he knew exactly what he was going to say—and that no, her opinion didn't matter at all.

'I think you've already made your feelings

only too plain,' he declared, leaning back against the pillows with his arms crossed behind him, his head resting on them. The movement made the sheet, all that covered him, slide lower at his narrow waist, almost exposing his hips, but unlike her he appeared totally unconcerned by his near-nakedness. Instead he looked totally at home—totally in control.

'I have?'

Domenico nodded his dark head.

'Would you be here if you hadn't? I don't remember forcing you to come to bed with me. In fact, I seem to recall that you were only too willing.'

'I...'

Alice tried to growl a protest then found she couldn't think of any way of continuing and she stared down at the sheet that covered her, her fingers moving restlessly to pleat the white cotton over and over on her knees. The glare she directed at the nervous gesture was the one she wanted to turn on Domenico, directing it right into his arrogant, smug face, but the knowledge of how she had been wrong-footed held her back.

Her own voice rang in her ears, the cries of

delight she had been unable to restrain, the moans of encouragement she had given him coming back to haunt her, now sounding like the worst reproaches, all the more embarrassing because she couldn't deny them even in the privacy of her own thoughts.

'Are you saying now that you didn't want to make love—?'

'No!' Alice flung out, cutting in before he could complete the sentence.

It was precisely because she had thought—foolishly, weakly, *stupidly*—that he might have been doing something close to making *love* that she had wanted it so much. But now that it was obvious she had been blindly deluded, there was no way on earth that she was going to admit to the truth.

What could she say?

*I thought you were here because you really cared for me. Because you realised that you didn't want that other woman. I thought you had come because you realised you missed me and that you wanted me back.*

Well, yes, he'd felt that all right but not in the way she'd been weak enough to allow herself to believe.

'I'm not saying that I didn't *want* you. Only that…'

Suddenly unable to stay where she was a moment longer, unable to bear lying here, like this, stark naked, beside an equally nude male, Alice pushed herself out of the bed, dragging the sheet with her, and reached for the white cotton robe that was hanging on the back of the door.

Ramming her arms into the sleeves, she pulled the soft material round her and belted the garment tight around her waist. It was a futile gesture, she knew, and far, far too late, but at least she felt better for being clothed, as if the robe provided some much-needed armour against Domenico's barbed remarks.

'Only that…?' came the pointed prompt from behind her, sparking wild anger, making her whirl round to him in a fury.

'Only that my wanting you sexually doesn't mean you own me!'

'I don't want to *own* you,' Domenico tossed back. 'And I don't recall ever saying that I did! But I am saying that I'm not yet tired of this relationship, that I still want you—and I'm damn sure you want me.'

'But I ended the relationship!'

'And I just restarted it.'

'You can't restart it—not without my agreement.'

With the haze of anger slowly fading from her eyes, Alice suddenly deeply regretted the fact that she had turned round. She hadn't thought that when she'd got up and taken the sheet with her, she'd also snatched away the only covering Domenico had. Not that he appeared to care— damn him. Instead he lay there, totally at his ease, as if only too aware of the glorious picture he made lying there, the golden skin seeming to glow in contrast to the white of the sheets, his long body fully relaxed and shockingly beautiful, almost spotlit by the shaft of sunlight that came through the bedroom window.

There wasn't an ounce of spare flesh on his muscular frame and he was everything a man should be. Strong, lean, shockingly handsome with those dark bronze eyes and black, black hair. His long limbs were arranged with a supreme elegance that showed them to their best advantage and Alice felt her throat dry at the memory of how it had felt to be held close to such male beauty, the feelings that had stormed through her at the touch of his hands, the kiss of that gorgeous mouth.

And she had only just let herself remember how much that feeling meant to her. She had given in to the longing she had felt and like an addict had returned to the source of her obsession. Only to regret it instantly and to wish she had never given in to the craving.

Because now she had to wean herself off it all over again. She had to endure once more the longing and the despair that being without what she most wanted could bring. She had been through it all once and had barely survived. Now she had to do it again—and this time it would be so much worse because she knew how hard it would be.

'Shouldn't you put some clothes on?'

Domenico's response was a nonchalant shrug that infuriatingly made Alice reflect on just how broad and strong his shoulders were, the impressiveness of muscle sliding under the tanned skin.

'I'd rather have a shower,' he returned. 'In fact I had hoped that we could have one together.'

'Hope away,' Alice retorted. 'That's something that's never going to happen.'

A faint smile greeted her angry outburst, one that only served to fan the flames of her irritation.

'You used to enjoy it. It was something we always did after—'

'Exactly! I *used* to enjoy it!'

She couldn't bear it if he said those lying words 'after we made love' once again.

'Past tense. It *was* something we *did*…'

'And something I would like to do again.'

Domenico was uncoiling his long body as he spoke, stretching lazily and getting to his feet. Having wanted him to move from his place on the bed, Alice now found herself wishing that he hadn't done any such thing. On his feet, he was too tall, too imposing, too *male* for the confined and very feminine space of her bedroom. The width of his shoulders blocked the sun from the window, casting a shadow over her face, and he was once again having to stoop slightly to avoid hitting his head on the sloping roof.

'But it's something I would *not* want to do again!'

'Why not?'

To her relief, Domenico had at least reached for his undershorts and trousers, pulling them on but leaving the waist and zip unfastened. Disturbingly, it didn't seem to make any difference to the heat of the blood in her veins, the heavy, sensual thud of her heart. Her fingers itched to reach out again and touch that smooth, golden skin and she had to cram them fiercely into the pockets of the white robe to keep them under control.

Oh, why had he had to mention those showers they'd shared? Showers that had been so much a part of every lovemaking session that they had been almost a continuation of the passion, rather than a cooling-off after it. In fact, more times than not they merged straight into another erotic encounter. The memory of the times they had made love up against cool, smooth tiles, with the warm water sluicing down on them, the scent of the shower gel in her nostrils, the bubbles foaming over her body, made her tremble in instant and devastating reaction.

'Is that something else you've decided is no longer any "fun"? Well, you'll have to forgive me if I don't believe you.'

Those deep-set eyes drifted to the bed, scanning the crumpled sheets, the disarray created by their passionate coupling such a short time before.

'Seems to me we had a lot of *fun*…'

Just what was going through this woman's head? Domenico asked himself. It seemed that she was changing her mood and her mind so often that it made his head spin. She had been so many different people since he had arrived at this cottage and not one of them had been the Alice he knew—or thought he knew.

No… Once more his eyes went back to the mess they had made of the bed.

There was one time, one place when she had been the Alice he knew—the Alice he wanted. In that bed, in his arms, she had been the woman with whom he had spent six glorious months. The woman who could make him want her just by breathing. Whose smile had an effect like setting a match to the fuse that led straight to his libido, triggering off an explosion in seconds.

The woman without whom his life and his bed had seemed so empty and cold ever since she had walked out on him.

And the woman who had so obviously been lying when she'd declared that their relationship was no longer any fun.

But she was equally obviously determined not

to admit to any such thing, damn her. For some hidden personal reason she was hell-bent on denying the truth, and for the life of him he couldn't see why.

Well, he was damned if he was going to let her get away with it. She was lying and one way or another he was going to make her admit that she was.

'Well, I hope it was enough *fun* to keep you satisfied for the rest of your life,' she snarled. 'Because, believe me, it's never going to happen again.'

'No?'

He almost laughed out loud at the furious indignation of her tone, the way that she drew herself up to her full height, the blue-eyed glare she flung right into his face. Couldn't she see that the very drama of the way she was behaving, the over-the-top reaction to everything he said, was making it impossible to believe her? It was a total contradiction to the way she had been in his arms, the wild, passionate creature she had been just a short time ago.

'You don't mean that.'

'Oh, don't I?'

That tone was enough to crush the urge to laugh, make him swallow his amusement down before it escaped. Laughter was not a good move at the moment. It would just make her angrier than ever, and that would just make sure that she wouldn't admit to whatever was bugging her.

Because something was bugging her. Something she wasn't yet prepared to admit to. But he would get it out of her. He was getting damn tired of her playing games, blowing hot and cold; a passionate sex queen one minute, an ice maiden the next.

'I meant it when I said I was leaving, didn't I? You didn't believe me then, if I remember rightly!'

That particular dig hit home, Domenico admitted. He hadn't believed her when she'd said she was going. He'd thought it was just a temporary storm, one they could easily weather. Then he'd come home to an empty house, an empty bed. Not even a note on the table.

'I don't know what the hell you do mean!' he exploded. 'You haven't even given me any sort of an explanation for why you walked out in the first place. One moment everything was fine, the next—'

'The next I found out about your other woman!'

'You what?'

It was so unexpected it hit him in the face like a slap. His head actually went back with the shock of it, his eyes narrowing sharply. She'd certainly meant that. It was there in her tone, in the way she held herself so stiffly upright. The stony-eyed look she'd turned on him.

'Explain that!' he rapped out. 'I want to know just what the hell you mean.'

Alice's chin lifted a shade higher, the muscles in her jaw tight and stiff. But her gaze didn't flinch from meeting his head on, the blue eyes colder now than they had been in the first moments after his arrival.

'What does the phrase usually mean? Don't tell me your English isn't good enough to understand.'

'Oh, I understand what it means all right, damn it!'

Domenico took a swift, angry step towards her, then thought better of it as he saw the way she was fighting with herself not to shrink back in the face of his advance.

'What I don't get is just what *you* mean.'

That determined, stubborn chin went even

higher. And her eyes flashed with a mixture of anger and rejection that told him that this time was real. That this time was something she was not about to change her mind over.

'I mean just two words,' she declared fiercely. 'And I'm sure even you will understand what they mean.'

Domenico leaned back against the window frame, crossing his arms across his chest.

'And those two words are?'

Alice took a deep breath, hesitated briefly then brought it out in a rush.

'Pippa Marinelli.'

*Pippa Marinelli!*

His thoughts spun, his brain seeming to short-circuit in a shower of sparks. He had tried to be so careful; he didn't want anyone finding out about his meetings with Pippa and jumping to conclusions.

He'd thought she would never know.

'How the hell did you find out about her?'

# CHAPTER FIVE

*How had she found out?*

A demand, Alice noted miserably; not a defence. Domenico hadn't attempted to deny the existence of Pippa Marinelli in his life. He hadn't tried to pretend he didn't know what she had meant by her accusation, or to say he didn't recognise the name.

Instead he had gone straight on to the attack with his biting query.

'Does it matter?' she managed, her voice giving way and breaking painfully in the middle of the question. 'Isn't it enough that I know?'

'Of course it matters.'

Domenico's eyes were blazing in cold rejection. The skin on his face seemed to have been draw tight over the stunning bone structure and his mouth had clamped tight into a cold, unyielding line. But then what had she expected? Guilt? Embarrassment?

He didn't look as if he had a guilty bone in his body.

'Then you should be more careful about leaving your mobile phone lying around.'

'You answered it? Read my messages?'

He didn't need to launch into a savage roar to show how furious he was at just the thought. His anger was there in the white marks etched around his eyes and his mouth, the deadly venom in the dangerously quiet voice.

'Of course not! What do you think I am? But I—I did pick it up. It must have fallen from your pocket or something—I found it under the bed. And the name—her name—was still on the screen.'

There had been other signs too. A letter, hastily pushed aside when she'd come to him in his office. Under other circumstances she might not have noticed but, with the missed phone call still in her mind, the swift glance that had caught the name 'Pippa' had alerted her suspicions.

She had tried not to connect the unknown woman's name with Domenico's frequent unexplained absences, and perhaps if things had been easier between them she might have succeeded.

But for weeks he had been difficult and unapproachable, rarely coming home until late, going out again early in the morning. The most damning evidence had been the reduction in the times that they made love. Some nights—many of them—she had been asleep before he came home. Or he had made some excuse that he had to work on something important, leaving her alone in the bed that then seemed so much bigger than even its king-size label merited.

And at the same time there had been so many swiftly broken-off conversations. Times when the phone had been put down as she came through the door, or when Domenico had said he couldn't talk right now but he'd ring back later.

'So you didn't talk to her?'

'No, I didn't—but would it have mattered if I did? I presume you'd have had some story ready—some cover plan! But you obviously weren't quite as discreet as you thought. People must have seen you—they were starting to talk.'

The faint pause was meant to give him a moment to say something—anything—and she fully expected him to use it to jump to his own defence. But Domenico didn't say a word.

Instead he stayed exactly where he was, with-drawn, unmoving, his expression as still and cold as if it had been carved from marble. Even the brilliant golden-brown eyes were hooded and unrevealing as he watched her face, obviously waiting for her to say more.

'Do—do you know what it's like?' she flung at him in the end, unable to bear the silence any longer. 'Do you know how it feels to be in a res-taurant—in the ladies' loo in an elegant hotel of all places!—and to hear three women gossiping about you? To hear them call you a poor, deluded, naive fool—a woman who doesn't even know that her partner's playing away—that he's been seen in there and in two other places with his latest squeeze—his new mistress, Pippa Marinelli?'

'You left me because of gossip?' The contempt in Domenico's voice threatened to flay the skin from her bones.

'Not just—'

'She isn't my mistress!'

It came low and hard and deadly. No hesita-tion. He didn't even attempt to raise his voice above a dark mutter, but he meant to be heard. There was no doubt about that.

Just as there was no room for doubt about the conviction in his tone, a conviction that cut straight through what she had been about to say and had her freezing into silence, her mouth still partly open, eyes wide, staring straight at him.

'What did you say?'

*You heard!* The dark scowl he turned on her needed no words to express his meaning, but all the same he still took the trouble to repeat what he had said, making it clear that he had no intention of being misunderstood.

'Pippa Marinelli is not my mistress. I don't give a damn what the gossips say. I don't care what amazing scenarios that wild imagination of yours has created—none of them are true. I'll say this only once more and then never again. Pippa Marinelli is not my mistress.'

There was no mistaking the conviction in his voice; in his face. Alice could have no doubt that he was telling her the truth. He couldn't be lying and meet her accusing glare with that steady, direct gaze. There was no deceit in those clear bronze eyes, nothing hidden or fake.

'Do you believe me?'

What else could she say? 'If you say so, then

yes—I believe you.' Though it tore at her heart to see the way his tight muscles relaxed, the faint smile that softened his mouth.

Two months before, yesterday perhaps, even an hour or so ago, she would have given the world to see that. She would have dreamed of being told that her suspicion about Pippa Marinelli was just fantasy, the creation of a combination of cruel gossip and awkward coincidences. Would have prayed to see Domenico here, with that smile on his face, knowing he could explain away her fears, put her mind at rest.

But it wasn't possible now.

Those dreams had been before Domenico had appeared on her doorstep with seductive words on his lips and a ruthless determination in his heart. Before he had enticed her into bed with the practised ease of a man who was used to getting what he wanted, whenever he wanted, and taken her blind foolish heart and used it for his own selfish purposes.

Before he had declared that she could only leave him when he gave her permission to go.

'I believe you,' she repeated, but it was a low,

despondent sigh rather than a confident statement of fact.

'Good.'

Domenico had pushed himself away from the wall, standing upright. He was about to come towards her, about to take her in his arms. She could see his intent in his face.

She had to stop him. If he touched her, she would be lost. And although it hurt like hell to do so, she forced herself to put up a hand to stop him.

'But if she's not your mistress then who is she?'

That stopped him all right. He stilled instantly, that smile fading in the blink of an eyelid, his expression hardening again, closing off from her.

'It's not important,' he said stiffly.

'It is to me.'

'It's none of your business. She's nothing to you.'

He caught the look she turned on him, the dark scowl growing blacker.

'I told you I'm not sleeping with her. What more do you want?'

Everything.

Nothing.

Alice didn't know which response to give.

It was the fact that he didn't see that was what mattered.

'You don't trust me,' he said.

'Trust was never the problem.'

And that was the truth; she saw that now. Pippa Marinelli had just been the last straw.

She had known for weeks—for months—that Domenico didn't really care for her. She had fallen head over heels in love with him and as a result had tumbled into his hands, his life—his bed—without hesitation and without thinking. And even when she had surfaced from the huge, heated pool of sensuality for just a brief moment, getting her head above water just enough to snatch in a much-needed cooling breath, a reality check, she had still not taken the time or the trouble to *think*.

She had just gone along with the delight of being in his company, being able to make love with him, sharing his life. Domenico had been all the world to her. It was only much later that she began to realise, slowly and painfully, just how small a part of his world she actually was.

'So what was the problem? No—don't tell me...' Cynicism dripped from every word. 'You weren't having *fun* any more.'

'That's right!'

Alice tried to make the words sound casual, even flippant. She'd picked on that line as as good an excuse as she was going to get for leaving when the truth was that leaving was the last thing she had ever wanted to do. It fitted with the person she had been trying to be—the person she'd thought that Domenico wanted her to be.

They'd met by accident when Domenico had come into the restaurant where she had taken a temporary job as a waitress. Back home, in England, she'd been a management trainee in a big clothing store but she'd hated it. Throwing the job up, she'd decided on a working holiday in Italy while she took the time to think about her life, about where she wanted to go, what she wanted to do. She'd got as far as Florence, and gone no further. She'd met Domenico and immediately had the feeling that she'd come home. That she'd found the whole point to her life.

Domenico, however, hadn't felt that way at all.

Oh, he'd been attracted to her from the start. He couldn't have made that any plainer. He wanted her in his life, in his bed—but he didn't want anything more. As far as he was concerned, she was there for relaxation: someone to be seen on his arm when they went out; someone with whom he enjoyed the blazingly passionate desire that had flared between them from the first moment their eyes had met.

But he didn't want anything more. Words like commitment, a future, *love*, didn't come into his vocabulary. Within a very few weeks, Alice had known that she wanted—needed more. But Domenico was quite content with what they had.

She'd tried, she'd really tried to go along with it, and for a while it had worked. But the more she had tried to squash down her emotional needs, the more they grew. She had tried to put on a brave face, to act as if she was having the 'fun' she'd told Domenico was all she was looking for, but inside she felt as if her soul was dying. The love that was supposed to fill her life had instead made her feel lost and empty and alone.

So when she'd heard the gossip about Pippa Marinelli, she'd seen it as a lifeline—or a kick in the pants. Something to bring her up short and make her realise just what she was doing to herself. Was she going to stay around, living this half-life, just waiting until Pippa Marinelli—or some other new flame in Domenico's life—superseded her?

Better to jump before she was pushed. At least that way she still had some pride left—and the wound of separation would be cold and quick and clean. So hopefully that way it would heal much more quickly.

The problem was that she hadn't reckoned on being pregnant.

*Pregnant!*

Oh, dear heaven, she'd actually forgotten why she had asked Domenico to come here in the first place! Events had caught her up, taken her so much by storm that she hadn't even had a moment to think about the truth.

But now she was forced to think of it, she had no idea what she was going to do. She had to tell Domenico about the baby; it was his child, after all, and as the father he had rights—if he wanted them. But would the Domenico to whom commitment was a dirty word want anything to do with fatherhood and all the ties that brought?

Always supposing she gathered up the courage to tell him. She had to tell him but she didn't know how. It would have been hard enough at the start, when he'd arrived in that stiffly distant mood. But this cold-voiced, cold-eyed monster who stood before her was something else again. That black fury that blazed in his eyes scared her so much that she didn't think she could even remember her own name if he'd asked her what it was.

'Our relationship had stopped being right a while before I left,' she managed, her tongue stumbling awkwardly over the words, perhaps because they were closer to the truth than anything she had said before. 'It wasn't what I wanted any more.'

'So how much *fun* did you want to have?' Domenico enquired now, each word as cold as steel, scorn sharpening them to a brutal knife edge.

She'd been restless that last couple of weeks, he reflected, looking back on the time after Alice had moved in with him. But he'd thought that it was just a temporary thing. It would pass. His time with Pippa had been so important; he'd assumed that Alice would still be there when everything was done. He'd been wrong.

'Where did we go wrong? Not enough parties?'

Her eyes actually widened in outrage as she turned them on him, that neat chin lifting again as she glared at him.

'It wasn't like that at all!'

'So what was it like, *bella*? What else should I have given you? More clothes? More travel?'

'I said—'

'Oh, I know what you said!' Domenico's hand came up between them in a wild, slashing movement as if cutting off any hope of a connection to her. 'Not what you wanted. But what *did* you want?'

What the hell was she holding out for? Surely she knew she only had to ask and he would give it to her?

'More money? Should I have given you a bigger allowance?'

'*No!*'

She actually looked appalled, her skin whitening over her cheekbones, her big blue eyes like dark pools.

Not money, then. It should have made him feel better to know that she didn't just see him as a bottomless wallet, a limitless credit card, but somehow it didn't. Just what the hell…?

Then suddenly he thought he had it. There was only one other thing this could all be about.

'Oh, I get it. Are you angling for marriage? Is

that it, Alicia, *cara*? You want a gold band on your finger?'

It looked as if he'd hit the target, right in the centre of the gold. For once she didn't have a word to say, and that was so unlike the Alice he knew that her silence might as well have been a clear, definite statement of fact. He'd caught her on the raw there, left her gasping for breath, unable to deny the fact that he'd hit home. It made his throat tighten, brought a sour taste to his mouth, to realise that she was, after all, going for the big one.

It was marriage or nothing, it seemed. That was why she had walked out on him. He was being held to ransom, and the price was a ring on her finger and his name on a marriage certificate.

'I told you—I don't do marriage, not ever. I thought I made that clear from the start.'

'You did.'

It was a strangled little voice, the words barely comprehensible, but Domenico was past caring. If she could deliver ultimatums, then he could too.

'There's only one thing that would ever make that a possibility and that's never going to happen…'

Something had changed in her face. A new expression had come into her eyes, a haunted, hunted look that gave him a grim sense of satisfaction to see it. His lovely Alice was finally beginning to realise that her dreams of becoming Signora Domenico Parrisi were just that—dreams. And they had no more hope of coming true than he had of claiming an English title and setting up home in a castle.

She had gambled all she had in her hand on the fact that if she walked out he would come after her and offer her anything she wanted just to get her back. Gambled and lost. OK, so he was here—he had come after her—but marriage wasn't on the table. And the fact was that he doubted if she'd really want it if she knew the whole truth.

So she'd played her trump card by making it plain that if he didn't offer marriage she wasn't staying around. But there was one important thing she hadn't reckoned on, one thing that could wreck her plan completely.

His eyes went back to the disordered bed, the covers still tangled and dishevelled in the evidence of the passion they had shared. A passion she had been every bit as unable to resist as he had. Cool, calculating Alice—an Alice he had to admit he hadn't even guessed existed— had made one fatal miscalculation when working out the odds.

Banking on the fact that he would be unable to stay away, she hadn't taken into account the possibility that she might not be able to control her own feelings quite as well as she had hoped. She had had him at her beck and call, but one touch, one kiss and suddenly all bets were off. She might not like it—she clearly didn't want to admit it—but she could no more resist him than he could control his passions where she was concerned. His cool, controlled Englishwoman wanted him so much that when they kissed every last trace of sanity flew out the window.

'What…?'

Alice seemed to be having trouble forming any words at all. Probably because she had just realised that she had no more cards to play. Her blue eyes looked faintly dazed with the shock of being outmanoeuvred, and she slicked a soft pink tongue over suddenly parched lips.

'What would that be?' she croaked, reaching out a hand to grab hold of a nearby chair as if she suddenly needed its support.

'Nothing either of us would want to even consider right now. I don't think we need to concern ourselves with anything more than the fact that I'm not looking for marriage, and if you're wise neither will you.'

'If I'm *wise*?'

She made it into a sound of disgust at the same time that it had a questioning note at the end.

'And just why would I need to be wise?'

'If you want this relationship to continue.'

Alice's breath actually hissed in between her teeth and her eyes sparked in irritation.

'I seem to recall that you were the one insisting that we stay together. If you remember, *you* were the one laying down the law and declaring that things weren't over until you said they were. I'd have been much happier if you'd stayed well away!'

'That's not what you were saying a short time ago.'

Once more Domenico's eyes swept over the disordered bed then up to Alice's white, tense face, noting the sudden burn of colour high along each cheekbone, the way that her teeth dug into the softness of her lower lip.

'With your body, if not actually in words.'

'What my body was saying…'

The tremor in her voice made the words break up, but the stiffness of the words, the tightness of that kissable mouth made it plain that it was a cold anger rather than any upset that made her tongue stumble. In fact he doubted if he had ever heard such a note of ice in her tone in all the time he had known her. He had definitely caught her on the raw with his comments about marriage.

'What my *body* was saying was that you're a sexy guy. I thought so when I first met you— and nothing has happened to change that opinion of you! You're an extremely attractive man and you must know that. There's no need for false modesty.'

It was almost a compliment, but that freezing tone, the flash of antagonism that turned the blue eyes almost silver warned him that it was meant as anything but. That look, combined with the way in which she had spoken, turned the phrase 'extremely attractive man' into something that was light-years away from the surface meaning, and made that 'sexy guy' sting like a dark insult.

'But I don't have to want a relationship with someone—or even to like them—to want to go to bed with them. I'm a woman, I have as much red blood in my veins as any man, and I have needs as much as the next person.'

'And my arrival just happened to coincide with a particularly—needy moment?'

Domenico didn't even recognise his own into-nation. But at least it accurately echoed the mixture of thoughts in his head—scepticism, scorn and sheer anger at the thought that he had been used uppermost in all of them.

'That's right.'

She even smiled as she said it but it was a cool, distant, brittle little smile, one that had no warmth or genuine amusement in it.

'And I think you felt the same way. I mean—have you found a replacement for me yet?'

'Have I…?'

The directness of the question actually stopped his thoughts dead just for a second. The next moment, shock was replaced by a rush of outrage that she should consider him so shallow, and so irresponsible.

'No, I damn well haven't! What the hell do you think I am?'

He wouldn't have thought it was possible but her second smile was even tighter and more distant than the first.

'Frustrated? Two whole months of abstinence— how wonderfully restrained of you! Then you'll know how I was feeling. It must have been mutual.'

'Just what—?'

'What am I saying? Do I have to put it bluntly? OK—I'll do that. It was a moment of madness, nothing more! But now that madness is over and I really should thank you.'

'Thank me?'

If Alice had turned into a furious cobra, spitting venom right into his face, he couldn't have been more appalled. He didn't recognise the ice-eyed, cold-voiced woman who stood before him. The total transformation took his breath away, scrambling his brains. Domenico reached for his shirt as a distraction and pulled it on. He started to fasten the first couple of buttons then abandoned the enterprise, leaving the rest undone.

'Yes, thank you! If I'd had any stupid ideas of thinking about taking you back, then you've made me realise just how foolish a decision that would be. To put it very bluntly, Domenico, you were an itch I had to scratch. But that was all. And now I'd be really grateful if you'd leave.'

'I don't think so,' Domenico declared, not moving an inch.

'And I don't *think*; I know,' Alice corrected pointedly. 'I know I want you out of here.'

Dark head high, long, slender back straight and stiff, she marched to the door and pulled it open.

'Now,' she added meaningfully when he didn't move.

But Domenico's attention had been distracted. Either the waft of air from the way she had stalked across the room, or one created by her pulling the door open so violently had caused a draught that had set a small pile of papers flying from their place on top of the chest of drawers. Floating in the air for a moment, they had blown partway across the carpet and come down to land on the floor almost at his feet.

And a heading on the topmost sheet had caught his eye.

Caught and held it in shocked disbelief.

'Domenico?' Alice suddenly became aware of his distraction—and the reason for it. 'I said I wanted you to— No!'

Abandoning her position by the door, she dashed forward, one hand outstretched to stop him just as Domenico bent to pick up the letter, his eyes fixed on the printed words.

'No!' she said but in a very different and much less assertive tone of voice.

'Yes…'

Domenico's own hand went out but towards her, with the aim of keeping her securely at a distance while he read and reread the words on the page before him. For a moment Alice struggled, fought to get free, to grab at the letter, but he clamped one big hand around both her wrists and held her still, his eyes on what he was reading.

It took some absorbing.

In fact, he had read it twice and still couldn't believe that he had actually seen what was in front of him.

Not that the letter was long. In fact, quite the opposite. It was short and to the point.

Very much to the point.

*Dear        Miss        Howard...appointment...
antenatal clinic...*

Antenatal clinic.

No matter how many times he read those
words, they still said the same thing.

Antenatal clinic.

'Are you...?'

He turned to glare at Alice, took one look at
her face and knew that the question didn't have
to be asked.

'You're pregnant!'

Alice had expected a roar of anger or some sort
of hostile reaction. This cold, calm—far too
calm—declaration of fact was unnerving. Its
very coolness, its total composure rocked her
sense of reality, knocking her mentally off
balance and leaving her floundering for words.

'This is a date and time for an antenatal ap-
pointment,' Domenico went on, as clinical as the
letter itself. 'You are pregnant.'

'I— Yes,' Alice managed, because there was
nothing else to say.

Abruptly Domenico released her hands, letting
them drop so suddenly that it jarred her shoul-

ders, adding physical discomfort to the mental distress she was feeling.

'Is it mine?'

His hands were busy, surprisingly so. He was buttoning up the rest of his shirt, fastening it across his chest, the action making it look as if he was closing it against her, creating a defensive shield against her.

'Of course. Who else's could it be?'

'How?'

For the tiniest moment, her shaken mind toyed with the idea of a flippant response. Something on the lines of 'Well, you know what we were just doing in that bed…?'

But even as she thought of it her throat closed up in panic at the anticipation of the way he would react, and she decided that it was much safer to take the question the way she knew he meant it.

'That time when I had the stomach upset. I took the Pill, but being ill must have—have affected how it worked. I'm not quite ten weeks…'

Just for a second, his dark eyes searched her face, probing deeply so that she had to struggle to meet that searing gaze. But then, just as she thought she couldn't bear it any longer, he gave a single hard, decisive nod.

'Mine,' he said with unexpected firmness, but somehow his easy acceptance of her assertion did nothing to set her mind at rest. He believed the baby was his, but instead of reassuring, his statement set every nerve tingling, lifting the tiny hairs all over her skin in a way that made her shiver in fearful reaction.

'Yes…' she began but her voice clashed with Domenico's.

'Mine,' he repeated on a very different note. 'I see.'

He wasn't looking at her. In fact, he was looking down and it took her a minute to realise that he was searching for his shoes. A moment later he had found them, stamped his feet into them without even troubling to find his socks, at the same time snatching up his jacket from the nearby chair.

'Domenico…' Alice tried but when he turned to her at the sound of her voice and she saw the wild blaze of fury in his eyes, her voice failed her completely and she froze into stillness and silence.

'You're carrying my baby—my child—and you never told me.'

'N-no—but...'

'And you would have let me walk out of here, without saying a word!'

*But that's why you're here,* she wanted to say. *That's why I asked you to come here. What I said we have to talk about.*

But to her shock and horror she was confronting the empty air. Without another word, Domenico had turned on his heel and marched across the room, disappearing out of the door before she had time to take in what was happening.

Still unable to move, she heard his heavy, rapid footsteps descending the stairs, the sound of the front door being wrenched open and then slamming shut again behind him.

It was when she heard the roar of the car's engine outside, the spurt of the gravel under the wheels as he put the powerful vehicle into gear and sped away, that she realised what had happened.

After all her failed attempts earlier to get him to go, it seemed that the revelation of her pregnancy had achieved just what she had wanted. But at precisely the point at which she hadn't wanted him to leave at all.

# CHAPTER SIX

WELL, if she faced facts squarely, Alice told herself as the afternoon faded into dusk, dusk into rainy, miserable night, she was no worse off than she had been at the start of the day.

When this morning had dawned, she had been living in this cottage, on her aunt's generosity, no job, no money, alone and pregnant.

She still was.

Nothing had changed. Domenico had blown in and out of her day like a fierce, icy hurricane. He had turned things upside down and inside out for a few brief moments, and then he was gone again, heading out of the door and driving off down the lanes as if all the devils in hell were after him. She was still in exactly the same position as she had been when she'd woken that morning. So why did it feel so much worse?

Because this morning, she had had hope. Oh,

she knew it had been a wild, foolish, totally unfounded sort of hope. But she had had a tiny thread of hope.

*Hope!*

Alice flung herself away from the window out of which she had been staring sightlessly as darkness fell over the little garden.

Hope? Who was she trying to kid?

She might have dreamed that Domenico would listen when she told him she was unexpectedly pregnant. That he would offer to stand by her, to help, to be there for the baby. But from the moment he had appeared things had started to go crazy. She had felt as if she was on a wild, whirling carousel, unable to get off. Every time she had thought to tell him the truth something had interfered or it hadn't seemed like the right time.

Now it seemed that there had been no such thing as the *right* time.

Domenico didn't do marriage, and his reaction just now showed that he most definitely didn't do fatherhood.

Slowly she smoothed her hand down over the front of the jeans and lilac T-shirt that she had dressed herself in again shortly after Domenico had stormed out. She had made herself do it, telling herself that if, just supposing, he changed his mind and came back again, she didn't want him thinking that she had been sitting here all that time, too miserable even to get dressed. It might have been close to the truth but she was determined that she wouldn't let him see that.

*If* he came back.

She'd still been fool enough to hang on to that tiny thread of hope. But not now.

Hope had gone right out of the window. She was on her own with this one.

Her hand slowed, stopped, curving protectively over her lower body. Over the spot where her baby lay, still only a tiny form, not even creating a bump to show its existence.

'It's just you and me now, sweetheart,' she whispered. 'Just you and me.'

But she'd take care of this child, she vowed to herself. It might not have been conceived in the best of circumstances, and her heart might ache desperately for the father who didn't want it— the man she loved—but she would love and care for his child as best she could.

And she'd start by having an early night. She'd take a cup of tea up to bed…

The sound of a car pulling up outside was so much something she had dreamed of in the loneliness of the afternoon that for a couple of seconds she refused to believe it was actually real. It couldn't be. It had to be something that her imagination had conjured up out of a longing that went so deep that she didn't dare even acknowledge it in her heart.

It wasn't happening…

But the slam of a metal door, the hurried stride of footsteps over the gravel could not be denied.

Halfway between the living room and the kitchen Alice froze, her heart thudding painfully high up in her throat so that she could hardly breathe. The handle of the front door turned, it was pushed open roughly, and Domenico strode into the narrow hallway, coming to an abrupt halt at the sight of her standing there.

He didn't say a word, and Alice found that she couldn't speak either. Her throat had dried, her tongue felt like a block of wood in her mouth, and all she could do was stare, unable to believe her eyes.

The wild weather outside had whipped his jet-black hair into disarray, spattering it with tiny diamond studs of raindrops. Similar drops of moisture spattered his face, looking unnervingly like the glisten of tears and spiking the thick, lush darkness of his lashes around those incredible eyes.

Tears? Domenico? Don't be stupid, Alice berated herself. Tears were another thing that Domenico didn't do.

The jacket he was wearing was unfastened and the wind had blown it wide open so that the rain had soaked into his shirt, plastering it against the hard, tight lines of his chest. She could see the golden tone of his skin, the black haze of chest hair through the saturated material in a way that made her wonder if he had been exposed to much more of the storm than just the brief walk from his car to her door. Certainly the heavy damp patches on his shoulders and sleeves seemed to indicate that he had been out of his car before this, and for quite some time. The black trousers clung soddenly to his muscular thighs too, and his shoes were spattered with mud.

He still had no socks on, she realised with a jolt to her heart. The glimpse of his ankles, which she could see between the hem of his trousers and those muddy shoes, were as bare as when he had marched out of her house several hours before. For some reason that realisation caught on something raw and sensitive deep inside her, making her gasp in sudden shock and pushing her into uncertain speech.

'D-Domenico...' she managed, cursing the inanity of it, the way that her voice shook in reaction to his sudden appearance. 'You came back.'

His beautiful mouth twisted in cynical response to the obviousness of her comment.

'I came back,' he echoed her words with a dark, mocking irony. 'As you see.'

'But—why? What are you doing here?'

'Isn't it obvious?'

The brusque, aggressive lift of his head dislodged a raindrop from the raven's-wing fall of his hair over the broad forehead and sent it splashing down onto his cheek. Domenico scrubbed at it with the back of his hand in an impatient, angry gesture, flicking the moisture off his fingers so that it fell against the cream-painted wall of the hallway.

'I've come back for my child.'

If he had shaken himself like a big black aggressive dog, until all the raindrops on his hair, his face, his clothes had sprayed over her in a cold shower, it couldn't have brought a rush of ice to her soul as quickly as his words. Alice felt as if some freezing hand had enclosed her heart in a cruel grip and was squeezing, hard and tight, taking all the life out of her.

He'd come back because of the baby she was carrying—but not because he cared at all about her.

'But—you can't have the baby without me…'

Domenico dismissed her protest with an arrogant, impatient wave of his hand. That was a small matter, the gesture said, and one that was easily dealt with.

'I know,' he said, hooded eyes clashing with her stunned, bewildered gaze. 'Of course I know that—that's why I've decided that we are going to marry.'

He'd known it was the only answer from the minute that he'd seen that damn letter. In fact, if his brain had been working properly he'd have proposed right there and then.

No, not proposed. Proposing meant asking,

giving the other person an option, presenting them with a choice and a chance to say no. He didn't intend that Alice should have any such choice.

Just as he had no other option in this matter.

There was no choice. They had made a child between them, and so everything else had to take second place. No child of his was going to grow up not knowing who its father was, as he had done. The baby had to have his name and so they had to marry. After that, they could take a breath; take a look at the situation.

He should have said that straight away. But just the fact of taking in what that letter said, and what it meant, had blown all his thoughts right off course. He had felt hunted, cornered, *trapped*. Only a few moments before he had been declaring that marriage was not for him; that, no matter how much Alice angled for it, manipulated things, she was never going to get a ring on his finger.

And then he had seen that letter and known that the only course open to him was the one he had been so angrily refusing.

He had felt as if his head was going to explode. He had had to get out of there. It was either that or tell her just what he thought; just how he felt.

And if he'd done that, there would have been no room at all for negotiation.

No matter how much it stuck in his throat, he had to open negotiations with this woman because she was the mother of his child. But the one thing that was non-negotiable was marriage.

Those were the thoughts that had come to him, the decisions he'd wrestled with in the hours since he'd walked out. He'd never actually gone very far away from the cottage— a few miles down the road, in fact. He'd parked the car and got out and walked and walked. He'd walked himself to a standstill. Until his thoughts were resigned and his heart had stopped racing.

He'd walked until he was as calm as he could be. And then he had come back here to tell Alice what he had decided.

'We are going to get married—and as soon as possible,' he said again, as much to make sure there was no going back as to convince her.

Because Alice wasn't looking at him the way he had expected. She wasn't looking anything like the way he had thought she would. Considering how much she had been angling for marriage earlier, this stunned, blank expression was the last thing he had anticipated. He'd been convinced that she would bite his hand off in her eagerness to take the wedding ring he offered. Instead she looked almost shocked. Almost as if she might actually say no.

'But you don't do marriage,' Alice said at last, and her voice sounded as rough as he felt, raw and off balance, totally uneven.

'I do when it's a matter of getting a legal claim to my baby. That *is* my baby you're carrying?'

'Of course it is! I told you that! I've never slept with any other man since I met you—I don't do that! And if you don't believe me—'

'I believe you.'

If he had had any lingering doubts at all, then the vehemence of her declaration drove them right out of his mind. Whatever else Alice might be—and right now he was beginning to wonder just how much he had ever known her at all— she was not the type to sleep around. He'd had one hell of a job to persuade her into bed with *him* so quickly, even though it had been blatantly obvious that she'd wanted to be there every bit as much as he'd wanted her. And once she was there, she had never looked at another man. That was why her sudden declaration that she was no longer having any fun and she was moving on had hit him like a ton of bricks.

Besides, there was something in her eyes, in her expression, in the sheer fury with which she had responded that convinced him that she was telling the truth. That and the dates told him that this baby was his.

'That's why we're getting married.'

'I don't have a choice?' Alice questioned sharply.

'No more than I have.'

'And what if I won't agree to marry you?'

*Don't be stupid*, the scornful glance he turned on her said only too clearly. *Of course you'll agree to it!* It was, after all, what she'd been angling for just a short time earlier. But perhaps she was determined to make him pay for the rejection he had flung at her back then.

Well, if she needed a little persuasion, he'd persuade. He supposed she was getting back at him for saying that there was no way he would marry her.

'I'll make it worth your while. I'll give you everything you want—anything you want.'

'Anything?' It had clearly made her think. 'Why?'

'No child of mine is going to be born illegitimate.'

He didn't realise how aggressive he had sounded until he saw the way her head came up, the uneasy step backwards she took. It twisted something sharply in his conscience, made him regret the shift in the balance of their relationship, but there was no going back now. He had set out on this path and he had too much to lose if he turned back.

But Alice was not giving in.

'I'll put your name on the birth certificate.'

'Not good enough,' Domenico stated ruthlessly, giving his dark head a fierce shake. 'It's marriage or—'

'Oh, you've changed your tune!' Alice mocked in a tone so brittle he almost wondered if speaking would snap it in two. 'A couple of hours ago it was no marriage, not ever! Now you can't seem to wait to get a ring on my finger! So tell me, marriage—or what?'

'Or I'll fight you.'

He waited just a nicely calculated moment as

he saw the statement hit home. Saw the way her face lost what little colour it had, the sudden wary apprehension in the beautiful eyes. He had her, if not exactly on the run, then certainly slowly starting to retreat.

'Can you risk a major legal battle? A drawn-out custody case? I'll bring in the best lawyers money can buy.'

'And you can afford the *very* best!' Alice flung into that shuttered, unyielding face.

'Of course.'

If he caught the sting of her sarcasm he didn't even acknowledge it by so much as a glance; not even the tiniest change in his expression revealed that her bitterness had hit home.

Suddenly Alice couldn't bear to be still any longer. She felt dizzy and faint, as if she had been standing in the glare of the sun for too long. Which, in a way, she supposed that she had. Facing up to Domenico was like being at the eye of a storm, struggling with something fiercely elemental. And she had been battling with him all day; a cruel, emotional battle that had taken its toll on her.

She couldn't face that harsh, predatory stare

any longer. Her legs felt insecure beneath her, shaky and weak.

'I—I have to sit down.'

Turning away hastily, she headed into the living room, stumbling slightly at the move from wooden flooring to the shabby carpet.

Behind her she heard Domenico mutter something, thick and raw in shock—and was that a note of concern that had sharpened his voice? She couldn't tell and she really couldn't even begin to think as her unwary movement made her head spin nauseously.

'Alice?'

He was close behind her, his hands fastening over her arms, taking her weight, supporting her as he half walked, half carried her towards the settee.

'Are you OK? Sit down... Can I get you something?'

Stunningly gentle for a big man, he guided her down onto the cushions, putting one hand behind her back, another at her head as she lay back. The room was spinning and she closed her eyes against the sensation.

'Here.'

She had barely noticed that he had gone but

suddenly he was back again, sitting beside her and holding out a glass of cool water. Alice took it and sipped gratefully, feeling the dizziness recede slightly.

'When did you last eat?'

Cool and sharp, Domenico's question went straight to the heart of the problem, making Alice feel very small and very stupid.

'I—I tried to have something at breakfast…'

Even as she said it, she expected—and got—his wordless sound of disapproval.

'*Idiota!* You must eat! You are pregnant.'

Of course. His concern would be for the baby.

'I felt sick and then…'

Then he had arrived and it seemed as if the world had gone crazy. She felt as if she had been picked up and whirled away from everything she knew, everything that kept her sane. And now she didn't know if she was on her head or her heels. One moment he was saying that he wanted her but would never marry her—the next he was insisting that they marry for the baby's sake.

Ah, yes—*for the baby's sake*. The thought of how little she actually mattered in all this slashed at her like a cruel knife and made a small, weak gasp escape her painfully dry lips.

'Relax!' Domenico had misunderstood the reason for her reaction. 'I'll get you something, then you'll feel better. What do you think you could manage?'

'Some toast.'

'And soup,' Domenico insisted. 'You need to eat something substantial if you've been fasting all day.'

'And soup,' Alice conceded, knowing it would do her no good to argue.

She really didn't think she could manage anything. Her stomach was so upset and the way that her nerves seemed to be tying themselves into tight, painful knots only added to the problem. She might be able to snatch a few quiet moments while Domenico disappeared into the kitchen but it would only be a brief respite. And somehow she had to think, had to try and find some way of coming to a decision about his proposal—his *demand* that she marry him.

But her thoughts wouldn't come together into any coherent form. Even though Domenico had left her side, she was still so sharply aware of him, just through the doorway in the tiny kitchen. She could hear him clattering about, opening doors, slamming them shut again.

Clearly he wasn't finding what he wanted as he muttered curses in explosive, frustrated Italian, and the sound of his fury at several inanimate objects brought a wry smile to her lips.

'The bread is in the wooden bin by the fridge,' she said into a rare moment of silence. 'And the butter in the—'

'Bread?' Clearly Domenico had found the remains of the small sliced loaf that was all the bread bin contained. 'You call this bread?'

The wooden lid banged down in a sound of disgust and another cupboard was opened— then another.

'And *where* will I find the toaster?'

Alice's smile grew. Something of the faintness was receding; enough to give her the strength to enjoy his discomfiture.

'There isn't one. You have to light the grill and use that.'

More expressive Italian issued from the kitchen. 'How the devil can you manage in such a place?'

'It's all I can afford. We're not all multimillionaires. Do you need me to come and help you with that?'

The outraged silence that greeted her question spoke more expressively of his indignation than anything he might actually say.

'I will manage, Alice. I do know how to cook.'

'You do?'

That was a surprise to her. She had lived for six months with this man but she had never learned that simple fact. In his city apartment, and at his villa outside Florence, he had always had a troop of servants to attend to his every need.

Her astonishment had shown in her tone and Domenico appeared in the doorway in response to her comment.

'I was not always a multimillionaire.'

'I know that. But—but you never actually wanted for anything.'

He had never talked of his past in any depth. Never let her in to any intimate secrets about his childhood or his youth, so it stunned her to find that he seemed prepared to do so now.

The black brows twitched together in a dark frown and the muscles in Domenico's jaw tightened, compressing his mouth as if he was determined to hold something back. But then, to her astonishment, he shrugged off the momentary hesitation.

'In my childhood I would have thought that this place was a palace,' he declared, making her jaw drop in genuine amazement. 'That is why I cannot believe that you would insist on bringing up our child in a dump like this when you know what I have to offer now.'

He might as well have thrown the knife he was holding straight into her heart. It wouldn't have hurt any more. Probably a lot less because the physical hurt was light in comparison to the emotional anguish that seared through her.

She'd been stupid enough to let her guard down, to forget just why he was here. But he had had no hesitation in reminding her of just what was uppermost in his mind—and it wasn't a concern for her welfare.

'So you think you can buy me?' she flung at him, pain making her voice colder than she had ever intended.

But it seemed that the accusation just bounced off Domenico's tough hide as if it was armour-plated.

'Not *buy, cara*,' he reproved with stinging gentleness. 'I merely suggested an arrangement that would suit us both.'

'But why does it have to be marriage?'

'I told you—no child of mine is going to be born illegitimate.'

'But that doesn't matter at all these days.'

'It matters to me.'

And there was no point in her arguing with that; no point at all. It was stamped into every hard line of his face, etched along each bone, each muscle in his body. Even the way he held himself told her that he was braced for a fight—for as long and as hard a fight as it took him to get what he wanted—and he had no intention of losing.

But how could she marry him; give up everything she was—her freedom—and go and live with a man who didn't love her? A man who only wanted her because of the precious baby she was carrying?

'Don't fight me on this, Alice,' Domenico said harshly, making her head spin in shock at the way it seemed that he had listened in to her thoughts and was now almost quoting them back at her. 'Because you won't win—you can't win. I want my child, and I'll fight you till the end of time to get it.'

Not waiting for her to answer, or even to attempt it, he turned on his heel and went back into the kitchen. A few moments later the savoury smell of soup crept into the living room, making Alice's ravenous stomach growl its emptiness.

Perhaps she could eat something after all. And perhaps, with something warm inside her, she might be able to think more clearly. Find some argument that would convince him she wasn't going to tie herself to a man she....

But that was where her thoughts floundered and came to a stumbling halt.

A man she...

It was no good. Try as she might, she couldn't force herself to say it even in the privacy of her own thoughts. Couldn't make herself say 'a man she didn't love'. Because the truth was the exact opposite.

She still loved Domenico.

She always had and she always would. She hadn't left him because she had fallen out of love with him, because she no longer cared, but because she adored him and she knew that he did not love her. She had never had any illusions that their relationship was for ever—and she had certainly never dreamed of marriage. She had fled because she'd feared that one day, and probably one day soon, Domenico would tire of her and she would find herself replaced by a newer model. And hearing stories of him with Pippa Marinelli had just been the last straw.

But then fate had conspired against her and she had found that she was pregnant. Or had that really been a gift from heaven? Because now Domenico had offered her marriage so that he could have his child.

What was she fighting for? She had always known that Domenico didn't love her; that hadn't changed. But so much else had. As his wife she would be part of his life, able to be with him every day. And perhaps that way, some time in the future, he might actually come to care for her.

And if he didn't, there would always be their baby. The child they had made between them. She had no doubt at all that Domenico would love the son or daughter he so clearly longed for, and she would love them both. It would be enough. It had to be enough—for now. She wouldn't hope for more—but nothing could stop her from dreaming.

'I make no promises about the soup.'

Domenico had come back into the room with a tray on which he'd placed a bowl and a plateful of toast.

'On the tin, they had the audacity to call it minestrone—but this looks nothing like any *minestrone* I've ever tasted.'

Setting the tray down on a small coffee-table, he moved it so that it was within reach of Alice, then flung himself down in the chair opposite, watching intently as she sat forward and picked up her spoon to eat.

'But I want to see you eat all of it.'

She would have a hard job swallowing anything with him sitting there, head back on the cushions, long legs stretched out in front of him, sockless ankles crossed. He gave an impression of being relaxed and at ease, but the long fingers of the hands that rested on the arms of the chair were moving restlessly, tapping out an impatient rhythm on the flowered fabric.

She didn't expect that he would wait very long before he went on to the attack again and she was proved right. She had barely got halfway down the bowl when he returned to the subject that was clearly uppermost in his mind.

'OK, how much is this going to cost me?'

'Cost?'

It wasn't the approach she'd been expecting. What she'd been dreading was another threat of legal action, of a court case that she couldn't hope to afford. So his talk of costs threw her off balance.

'What sort of a settlement would make the idea of marriage appeal?'

'I don't want a settlement.'

*Porca miseria*, but she was stubborn! Domenico cursed to himself. Stubborn and totally unpredictable. He could have sworn that she had been angling for a ring on her finger with this damn running-away business, the whole 'not having fun any more' blatantly a cover-up for something else. But now that he had *offered* marriage, she'd tossed it back in his face as if it was the last thing she wanted.

'Alicia, a marriage between us could work in other ways than just the fact that we are going to become parents. I'm not proposing just some marriage of convenience.'

He had her attention now. The spoon had

paused, halfway to her mouth, and she was staring at him, watching him like some wary animal suddenly caught in the headlights.

'We would have a real marriage. You would be my wife—in my home, in my life…in my bed.'

That spoon was moving again, but not towards her mouth. Instead it was slowly put down again, into the bowl, the handle resting against the side.

She was definitely listening now so he pressed home his advantage.

'And surely what happened between us here today tells you that we could be good together—great together.'

'In bed?' It was a strangely rough-edged question but at least it was not the determined, cold-eyed refusal he'd met with before.

'In bed or out of bed. I told you, *mia bella*, you may have tired of our relationship, but I have never grown tired of you. I still want you, as much as, if not more than, when we were together.'

Alice opened her mouth as if to speak, but no sound came out. He watched her fight with the moment of weakness, saw the elegant lines of her throat move as she swallowed hard.

'You do?'

Domenico's laughter was low and sceptical. Did she doubt it? How could she doubt it?

Sitting forward, he leaned towards her, his arms resting on his knees, his fingers spread in an open gesture. His eyes locked with her uncertain blue ones, seeing the dark pupils, the wide-eyed stare, the long, curving lashes.

'Did you listen to a word I said earlier? Didn't what happened in your bed tell you anything? I want you—and I want our baby—and I'll do whatever it takes to make sure that our child is born into a legitimate marriage.'

'Why is that so important to you? I'd give you access…'

She broke off abruptly, blinking hard in shock, as he shook his head in adamant rejection of her tentative suggestion.

'No?'

'No. Access isn't good enough, Alice. I want marriage.'

'But why? Tell me why it has to be this way. You can't expect me to marry you if you don't.'

She didn't know what she was asking. No one had ever delved so deeply into his life, or come so close to things he had kept hidden. He had never let any woman open up that part of him.

But if it meant getting his child—being a father to his son or daughter—and getting Alice into the bargain, having this woman in his bed every night...

'Dom?'

*Dom.*

It was the name she had once said with such warmth—with such affection. She'd used it in passion too, in a husky whisper in his ear at the most intimate of moments as he'd taken her as his own, sheathing his hungry body in her welcoming warmth. And she'd cried out in ecstasy as she came, keening his name on a long, drawn-out sigh.

*Dom.*

He had given no one else the right to use that name. And hearing it now seemed to crack something open inside him, bringing him hard up against the fact that it was let her in—or lose her. Lose his rights to her and the child, except for what she would allow him.

Unable to keep still, he pushed himself out of his chair, turning towards the window and staring out at the dark night where the rain was still falling, lashing against the glass, whirling in the wind. He didn't know where to start or how to say it. He had kept it to himself for the thirty-four years of his life.

But then she said it again.

'Dom?'

And that brought him whirling round, seeing her upturned face, those blue, blue eyes watching him. Watching and waiting for an answer.

Abruptly he held out a hand to her. And she took it, letting him pull her upright, draw her close to him.

Still holding her, looking deep into her eyes, he let his free hand rest on her body, low down, where his child was beginning to grow.

'My parents are both dead.'

She knew that much already. He had told her at the very beginning of their relationship that he had no mother or father.

'I have no other relatives.'

Alice's tiny gasp escaped her involuntarily.

'None?'

'No one.'

'Not a cousin or…?'

'No one.'

His hand moved, fingers splayed across her belly.

'This child—our baby—is the only other living person in the whole world who has my blood in its veins. I want that child—my child—to have my name.'

It was only part of the truth, but he prayed it was enough to satisfy her. The rest he had never told anyone, and would willingly go to his grave without ever speaking of it.

'So tell me what it will cost me and I'll pay any price.'

Her silence seemed to drag on for an eternity. But then, at last she slicked a moistening tongue over her dry lips and drew in a long, slow breath.

'Just marriage,' she said, so softly that he barely caught it and thought he hadn't heard right.

'What?'

He ducked his head until her mouth was close to his ear. In this position he had nowhere to look but at the swell of her breasts, rising and falling with the unsteady, rapid rate of her breathing. The scent of her skin was both a delight and a torment to senses that were already over-stimulated, nerves that seemed tight with too much tension.

'What did you say?'

'Just marriage,' Alice repeated, still in a whisper, but more firmly this time. 'All I want is marriage.'

'You'll marry me?'

And ask for nothing more? It seemed impossible.

But she was nodding silently, her head down, her eyes closed. Nodding agreement.

'Yes, I'll marry you,' she said, making sure there could be no mistake.

Suddenly she flung up her head and looked him straight in the eye.

'But Pippa Marinelli...'

'Pippa Marinelli is no threat to you,' he hastened to reassure her. 'You will never have to hear about her again. I swear to you.'

Slowly Alice nodded her head again, this time more confidently.

'In that case, I'll marry you and we'll raise this child together.'

Domenico was thankful that her upturned head offered him her mouth, suggesting without words that they seal their bargain with a kiss. A handshake didn't seem quite appropriate, for all that it was a business agreement they had finalised, for a marriage that was all formality and nothing of feeling, except that they both cared for the child that was to be born to them.

It was as he angled his head to take the kiss that the kick of reality hit, landing hard in the pit of his stomach.

*Just marriage.* Of course.

*Just marriage* was quite enough for any woman. *Just marriage* gave her the rights to half of everything he owned. She didn't have to name her price for agreeing to his terms—it was right there in her statement.

Just marriage.

But then their lips met and in the sensual explosion the sensation sparked off he managed just one thought before his mind went into total meltdown.

He didn't care. He didn't give a damn at all.

It was worth handing over half of everything he owned to have this woman back in his bed, and to know that she was bringing his child into his life.

# CHAPTER SEVEN

PRECISELY two weeks ago, at exactly this time of night, she had been standing at a window, staring out at the dark garden. Now she was doing just that again. But the view that met her eyes and the circumstances in which she found herself couldn't be more different.

Then the garden had been tiny, windswept and rain-soaked, and she had been under cooler skies at her English cottage. Now she was looking down at the extensive grounds of Domenico's elegant Italian villa, after a day of warm sunshine and blue, blue skies.

And tomorrow was her wedding day.

Out there, beyond the window, still visible because of the lights that lined the long, sweeping drive, workers were still making sure that the gardens were immaculate and the huge ornate fountain in perfect working order, ready for the big day. Downstairs, in the villa's huge ballroom, the floral decorations were being set up and the tables prepared for the reception after the ceremony in the morning. They were to be married in the village church and then come back to the Villa d'Acqua in a horse-drawn coach that had been freshly scrubbed and painted, ready to transport her and her new husband to their marital home.

'My husband...'

Alice whispered the words under her breath because she still couldn't quite believe this was actually happening.

This time tomorrow she would be Signora Domenico Parrisi. She would have Domenico's ring on her finger and they would be man and wife.

And her baby would grow up knowing its father. Knowing it was loved.

'Loved.'

Alice winced away from the stab of pain that just saying that word brought to her. It was impossible to think of her coming wedding without wishing that it could be perfect in every way. But perfect would mean that she had Domenico's love. And that was the one thing that tomorrow's wedding would be lacking.

She couldn't fault her husband-to-be in anything else. In the two weeks since she had said she would be his wife, he had taken care of everything—dealt with every need she might possibly have and a few that hadn't even crossed her mind.

He had taken charge immediately, organised everything, taken every last responsibility from her, and all she had had to do was to pack a small case with the things she needed to settle herself into the villa—and plan the dress she was to wear for the wedding.

Even there, Domenico had made things easy for her. A designer had been contacted, summoned to the villa. She was to choose anything she wanted—exactly what she wanted—and it would be provided for her. Now the most beautiful dress, the dress of her dreams, hung in the dressing room, carefully shrouded in protective plastic, waiting for her to put it on tomorrow morning. And tomorrow her father would walk her down the aisle.

Domenico had arranged that as well, contacting her parents in New Zealand where they now lived, arranging first-class flights for them—and for all her friends—so that they could be here, with her on the big day. He had never put a single foot wrong.

And perhaps that was the reason for her uneasiness and edgy feeling tonight, Alice told herself as she moved away from the window, wandering restlessly about the large, elegant room. Domenico had been polite, considerate, generosity itself, but he had always remained—well, the only word she could come up with was...

*Distant.*

From the moment that he had had her answer to his proposal—his demand that she marry him, from the time that she had said yes, she would be his wife, he had totally withdrawn from her so that at times he no longer seemed like the same man. His courtesy was impeccable; he had done everything he could to make sure she was comfortable and had everything she needed. But it was as if someone had put up a glass wall between the two of them, with each on different sides, so that they could see and hear each other, but not reach out. Not touch.

Except where the baby was concerned.

Oh, yes, where the baby was concerned Domenico was all interest, all attention. The first thing he had done when she had agreed to marry him—even before he had started any arrangements for tomorrow's marriage ceremony—was to arrange for the best medical care that money could buy. She had been examined, assessed, had every blood test known to medical science. And only then had Domenico agreed to let her travel to his home outside Pavia to join in the wedding preparations.

A light tap at the door brought her head round quickly, a movement she regretted as it made her head spin. This had happened several times in the last few days, something she put down to her non-stop tiredness and the persistent nausea that dogged her days.

'Come in,' she said but Domenico had already opened the door and was halfway into the room.

'I told you to rest,' he said reprovingly as soon as he saw that she was not, as he had instructed, lying down with her feet up.

'I was too nervous to sleep,' she admitted. 'There's so much to remember—so much to do before tomorrow.'

'And none of it that you need to trouble your head with. Everything's under control. But you have been looking tired—you're too pale. And you barely ate a thing at lunch.'

Did he notice everything she did—or didn't do? He must have eyes like a hawk, because she had been convinced that she had made a fair pretence of eating the light meal served to her. And she had thought that Domenico had been intent on talking to her father so that her non-existent appetite would go unobserved.

'It's this sickness.' She grimaced wryly. 'They might call it morning sickness but it doesn't just appear in the morning! If it did, I might be able to cope. As far as I can see, it's all-day sickness really.'

'And you've been overdoing things.'

His hand came up to touch her face, smoothing a long finger across the top of her cheek, and her heart seemed to stand still suddenly at the un-expectedness of his touch.

He had barely come near her in the two weeks since he had proposed this marriage, and in spite of his protestations that he wanted her more than ever before he had made no move to take her to bed or even to show any sign of warmth towards her. In fact she had become so used to him keeping a strict distance between them that it had rocked her sense of balance when, arriving back from the airport, where he had collected her parents from their flight, he had greeted her with an apparently affectionate kiss on the cheek.

It had taken a moment for her to realise that it was precisely because of her mother's smiling presence just behind him that he had even made the gesture. They were to act as if this marriage was a real one, he had told her. No one was even to suspect that they were marrying for any reasons other than the fact that it was a perfect love match. And so of course he had put on an act, setting out to impress his potential in-laws from the start.

'You have shadows under your eyes,' he said now, the sharpness of the words crushing down the weak rush of hope that his touch had been a caress and not the criticism it had turned out to be. 'And you're losing weight.'

His hands came round her waist, measuring it against the span of his fingers, and his frown said that he was not at all pleased with what he saw. Alice didn't need any tape measure or scales to tell her how the weight was dropping off her.

She felt so sick all the time that it was a constant struggle to eat, and when she did manage to swallow something, it didn't always stay down. She'd hoped that as she got further into her pregnancy the nausea would wear off, but, if anything, the past two weeks had been worse.

'Well, it's just as well I'm not putting on too much or I'd never get into that outrageously expensive dress I'm planning to wear tomorrow.'

Alice tried for lightness, but knew that her attempt to soften his mood even a little had failed when she saw his black brows twitch together in a dark frown, his features freezing into such a hard expression that she felt her attempt at a smile might actually bounce back off its rigidity and hit her in the face like a reproach.

'It doesn't suit you,' he snapped coldly. 'And it won't be good for the baby. You really should take better care of yourself.'

'Better care of your son or daughter, don't you mean?' Alice flung back, the stinging pain of rejection so sharp that she couldn't even try to hold back her reproach. 'I'm surprised that you even notice I exist, except as the incubator in which your precious heir is growing!'

'Oh, I notice all right,' Domenico snarled irritably. 'I can't help but notice—and I don't like what I see. You don't look strong enough to stand on your own two feet, let alone nurture a child. How would you feel if something happened—?'

'How would *you* feel if something happened, you mean!'

Alice pulled herself away from his restraining grasp, unable to bear his critical gaze, the dark reproof in his frowning eyes. 'After all, that would mean that you'd wasted your time and money—and married me for nothing!'

Domenico's reaction was not what she expected. That dark frown was replaced by a cool, assessing narrowing of his bronze gaze. And his response was low and fast as a striking snake as he demanded, 'Is that what you want? To call the wedding off? Are you going back on your word?'

It was only what he had been expecting, after all, Domenico reflected. He had pushed her into this marriage for his own reasons, offering her nothing but financial security in return. Perhaps she was now regretting her decision, wishing she had chosen that 'fun' she'd said she wanted.

Certainly that seemed possible from the way that she was hesitating over her answer now.

'Is that it?'

'No.' Her response was low, but firm. 'No, that's not what I want. I said I'd marry you and I will. After all, who would turn down a chance to become mistress of all this?'

The wave of her hand took in the luxurious room furnished in cream and gold, the adjoining dressing room and *en suite* bathroom, and beyond the windows the expanse of the beautiful grounds sweeping right down to the banks of the river that had given the villa its name.

'You needn't worry that I'll jilt you at the altar. I'll be there tomorrow, never fear. That is, if you still want me.'

If he still wanted her! *Dio*, was the woman blind? Didn't she know what it did to him just to be near her, the way that his body responded instantly to her presence, the raging desire that scrambled his thoughts in seconds? The need that he had had to clamp down on since that day in her cottage? That he had had to bury in concern for her well-being?

She had looked so pale, so ill from the first

moment that he had brought her here. At first he had thought that it was the after-effects of the journey, but she hadn't seemed to pull round very quickly. If anything, she had looked worse, more fragile, with every day that passed.

Her hand moved, lightly covering the spot where his child lay.

'If you still want us,' she amended softly.

'Of course I want you. What man wouldn't want a beautiful woman as his wife and the prospect of his first-born child arriving just a few months from now?'

'First-born?'

He wouldn't have thought that it was possible for Alice to look any paler; her skin was almost translucent as it was. But as she echoed his words it seemed that even the faintest wash of rose fled from her cheeks and her eyes were smoky with shock as they stared into his face.

'*First*-born?' she repeated. 'I don't recall agreeing to any more children.'

'And I thought you understood that this was to be a real marriage—not just a business arrangement.'

'Real—for how long?'

Did she really believe that all he wanted was her name on a marriage certificate and then she was free—free to have fun, he presumed?

'For as long as it takes,' he stated bluntly. 'I want my child to grow up in a real family, with two parents—brothers and sisters if possible.'

'Are—are you saying…?'

'I'm saying that when I make those vows tomorrow I mean to keep them. This isn't going to be just a show marriage, Alicia, *cara*. I will be a father to my child—and a husband to you.'

'You're surely not saying—t-till death do us part?' she managed in a whisper.

'I'm certainly not looking at any temporary arrangement.'

'But—we don't love each other.'

'Love!'

Domenico couldn't hold back the cynical laughter that escaped him at the word. Was it love that had brought him into the world? It had been more of another, very different, four-letter word. He had been created by lust, pure and simple—not that there had been anything *pure* about a quick, sordid and rough event.

'And do you believe in "love"?' he questioned

sharply. 'Is there really such an emotion? And what makes you think that any marriage based on *amore* has any better chance of lasting than one grounded in sound, practical reasons for its existence?'

'Practical?'

Somehow she managed to make the word sound like the greatest insult possible.

'Surely you're not deluding yourself with some dream of a happy-ever-after with the one love of your life? You must know that that is only an illusion of songwriters and fantasy novelists. Arranged marriages have worked very well for centuries—and often with less between the participants than we have.'

'And we have…?'

'Oh, *mia bella*—don't pretend that you have to ask! You know what we have. We have this…'

He caught her wrist, drawing her gently towards him. Sliding one hand under her chin, he lifted her face to his and bent his head to take her lips softly. He had to fight to hold back on the hot passion that flashed its way through his body as his mouth touched hers, crushing down the need to snatch her up in his arms and carry her over to the bed, flinging her down on the gold-coloured coverlet...

And she didn't help matters because after a tiny heartbeat of hesitation, the briefest snatching in of a breath, she just melted into him, her mouth clinging, opening softly under his, her sigh tormenting him with its sound of surrender, just when he knew he must not act on it.

Her hands came up around his neck, sliding into the dark hair at the back of his skull, smoothing, stroking. The softness of her breasts was crushed against his chest, and the slender curve of her hips was cradled by his pelvis, heating and hardening his body in an instant so that it was impossible she couldn't feel the power of his hunger for her, the rigid force of his need.

In spite of himself, his arms came tight round her, crushing her to him, but as soon as they did so, he felt the thinness of her, the delicacy of her frame, the fragility of her bones. And she was all bone. So finely spun that he feared that if he used even one small part of his strength to hold her, she might actually crack into a thousand tiny pieces.

'Dear God, *cara*,' he muttered against her lips. 'Don't do this to me—don't—*stop*!'

He regretted the word as soon as it had escaped him; regretted the force of the command, the instant effect that it had on her.

She froze in his arms, her dark head bent, resting against his chest, eyes hidden from him. But there was a new tension in the slender form, one that held her totally distant from him even though she was still standing so very close.

'I thought…you wanted…'

Her voice was muffled against his shirt but he thought he could hear the thickness of tears in her stumbling words. And when he gently brought her head up so that he could see her face, those deep blue eyes were sheened with moisture that she tried vainly to hide, struggling to pull her chin away from his firm, restraining grip.

'I *want* you,' he assured her deeply. 'Never doubt that. I've never wanted any woman more.'

She tried for a response, that soft pink mouth opened, worked, but no sound came out. And so Domenico bent his head, risking a brief, delicate kiss, shuddering faintly as he endured the stinging pulse of primitive need that tormented his yearning body all over again.

'But don't you have a tradition that the groom

must sleep apart from his bride on the eve of their wedding night?'

'It's supposed to be bad luck if they don't,' Alice agreed, her tiredness showing in her tone, which was flat and lifeless. No emotion in it at all.

'Then we don't want to risk that. Besides, you look worn out. The preparations for the wedding have taken it out of you. You need to rest—take care of the baby.'

'The baby,' Alice echoed, but she nodded slowly. 'I could do with an early night.'

'You have one.'

Domenico dropped a kiss on her forehead, easing himself away with a care that was as much to appease the screaming protest from his own aroused body as to make Alice feel that he was not keen to leave. If he didn't get out of here fast, then he would never leave.

He'd fought the need to hold her, to kiss her, to *have* her for as long as he could. He wanted to give her time and space and consideration, but he was only human. If he stayed a second longer with her in his arms, with the soft scent of her skin mixed with some subtle rose-based perfume tormenting his nostrils, weaving through his thoughts like warm, intoxicating smoke, then he would not be able to hold out any longer.

The temptation that the big, soft, inviting bed offered was almost more than he could stand. He was going *now*—*pronto*—before he did something damn stupid. Something he would always regret.

'It will be a long day tomorrow,' he said, ruthlessly erasing every note of regret from his voice. 'But when we're man and wife there will be a lifetime of nights we can share. Goodnight, *cara*. I'll see you in church.'

A lifetime of nights, Alice repeated in her thoughts as she watched him walk away from her and out of the room. Never once did he hesitate or look back, and he closed the door so firmly behind him that he might have been going away for good; never coming back.

*A lifetime of nights we can share.*

But tonight was the night that she needed him. The one night that would have meant so much. The night when, if he had stayed, if he had held her in his arms, kissed her, taken her to bed, she might have been able to feel that he wanted her, really wanted her, for herself.

Not just as the prospective mother of his

child—of his 'first-born'—and the potential breeder of the brothers and sisters he wanted this baby to have, but as Alice. As the woman he said he wanted but who, once he'd had her agreement to marry him and his ring on her finger, he hadn't even touched since she had come into this house.

Until tonight.

Tonight he had at least held her. He'd kissed her. But when she'd made it plain that she would love to take things further he had removed himself, disentangling himself from her clutching hands and putting her carefully aside. Oh, he had been gentle, considerate, courteous even. But he had not wanted to make love to her.

*Because she had to take care of the baby.*

Alice sighed, deep and low, blinking back tears as she rubbed at her back, where tired muscles ached miserably. Domenico was right, of course. She was worn out, and she hadn't been feeling well for days.

But the fact that he was right didn't make things feel any better. If anything, they made them worse. He was right—and he had thought of her as the mother of his child, taking care of her

needs, concerned for her health, her strength—
and for the baby!

'And I wanted him to care for *me*!'

She wished he had felt so overwhelmed by his
feeling for her—even if it was only physical—that
he had not been able to tear himself away and had
taken her to bed, to lie with her through the long
hours of the night, and wake at her side on the
special morning that tomorrow was going to be.

She didn't give a damn about bad luck! It
was only superstition, and she didn't believe in
superstition.

The truth was that for Domenico tomorrow
wasn't going to be such a special day at all. He
might talk about a *real marriage,* about spending
a lifetime together, about having more children
after this precious baby who had brought him to
the altar when it was the last thing he had
planned and the last thing he had wanted.

But he had shown no feeling about it. In fact
he had said straight out that he didn't believe in
love, stating openly that he wanted a practical,
arranged marriage and had only chosen her
because she was pregnant with his baby.

But how could she fault a man who cared about

his unborn child as deeply as Domenico so obviously did? She had felt the heated hardness of his body when she'd cuddled close. She recognised, though he would hate it if he knew, the struggle that he had had to pull away from her, the fight he had had not to give in to the passion that flared between them. How could she not recognise it when it was the same primitive need that had racked her too? She didn't possess Domenico's ruthless self-control, his unyielding determination, and would have given in to it if he had not decided for her.

And the truth was that she was tired, bone weary, with that hateful nausea making her stomach roil, her head spin.

But oh, how she wished he had stayed.

When he was here it all seemed easier. She could even ignore the sickness to a degree, drawing strength from his big, strong, comforting presence; feeling his arms around her for support.

Now that he was gone she felt doubly bereft, lonely, lost—and ill. And she didn't know how she was going to get to sleep.

She'd run a bath. A deep, deep, warm bath. And she'd soak in it for as long as she could, lying there in the soothing water, feeling it ease away the aches in her back, the uncomfortable twinges that seemed to be coming and going all over her body. She'd linger until she felt relaxed enough to sleep—until she was too tired to do anything else—and then she'd crawl into bed and hope that oblivion would claim her and keep her from thinking, or from dreaming, until the morning of her wedding day dawned.

The bath worked. Or perhaps it was just the sheer exhaustion that overwhelmed her, dropping her suddenly into total blankness almost as soon as she lay down and closed her eyes. She knew nothing, felt nothing for hours, lying dead to the world as the night slipped away and the morning came closer.

Until something invaded her sleep and brought her rushing awake with a jolting shock.

She didn't know what had happened; what nightmare had invaded her sleep and forced her to open her eyes. But it had to have been something dreadful because she found herself sitting half-upright, staring straight ahead, heart racing, her shaking body slicked with sweat as if she had been running from some appalling horror.

'Oh, help…' she groaned, rubbing a trembling hand across her face to drive away the sleep demons that had pursued her into her dreams.

And as she did so it happened again.

And it wasn't a nightmare, or a fantasy demon. It wasn't anything imaginary at all.

The monster that had grabbed at her, pulling her out of sleep and into the dreadfully cold light of the dawn, was a cruel, physical, painful reality.

It came as a savage wave of dizziness, a shuddering nausea and an agonising, brutal cramping sensation that had her hand flying to her abdomen in shock.

'Ooof!'

The sound was pushed from her as she held her stomach, gasping in pain, her mouth wide open, breath catching in her throat.

*'Ouch!'*

For a couple of seconds that was all she could manage—simply handling the pain took all the strength she had. It was as the cramping pain subsided, leaving her panting and weak, that some ability to think returned and with it the devastation of realising just what was happening.

'No! Oh, *no!*'

The baby…

She couldn't…

Oh, no, please, *no*! Not the baby.

The receding pain gave her the momentary strength to fling herself out of bed, stand upright, though her head whirled sickeningly and her eyes blurred into sightlessness.

Domenico.

His name was the one clear, focused thought inside her panic-stricken mind.

Domenico—she had to get to Domenico. He would know what to do. He would be able to get help, he would—

'Ohh… Oh!' she gasped as another wave of pain attacked from out of nowhere.

By the time it had subsided again she was sweating hard and breathing rawly. Her legs were trembling badly, barely supporting her, but she forced herself to move, stumbling across the carpet and out into the long, dark corridor.

Domenico's room was just a few doors down, directly opposite the huge suite that would be theirs when they were married.

*If* they were married. Because surely this…

Another clutch of pain destroyed her thought

processes, taking with them any hope of following through on what she had been wondering. Instead she wilted against the wall, grateful for its hard support at her back as she panted her way through the agonising contraction, her concentration too fierce to allow her to think of anything but that.

And that was something for which she was thankful when her brain started working again. Because thinking hurt too—bringing with it the anguish of knowing that there was only one possible reason for this terrible pain.

'Domenico…'

It was muttered through teeth gritted against the fear and the horror, her jaw tight with determination to get to his room, to get to him.

'Domenico…'

Her feet dragged, every step was an effort, but eventually she made it to the door, her fingers reaching for the handle.

She didn't have time—didn't have the strength—to knock and wait, and she could only summon up the energy to swipe a perfunctory slap of her hand on the wooden panels as she turned the handle, tried to push it open.

For the space of a couple of agonised heartbeats, she thought that it was not going to move, that it was locked against her, but then, just as a despairing moan rose to her lips, she felt it give, fly inwards, taking her with it.

'What the—? Alice?'

It was Domenico's voice, harsh with shock, but, her eyes blurred with panic, Alice couldn't see where it was coming from until, blinking frantically, she managed to focus her vision better.

Her first thought was a sense of shock that the room wasn't in the semi-darkness of the dawn as she had expected, but filled with the bright light of the several lamps that were burning.

The next was that Domenico was not in his bed. Instead he was up—and fully dressed, dark and devastating in a black T-shirt and jeans.

Had he too been unable to sleep? she wondered, briefly diverted, her whirling mind latching on to any distraction from the blackness of reality.

'I'm sorry—' she tried, only to have the words snatched away from her by another vicious crush of pain. *'Dom!'* His name was a high, desperate cry of panic.

*'Alicia, carissima—tesora—cosa c'e che non va?'*

Domenico was coming towards her, his hands out to her, his face white, all his English deserting him in his shock.

'Oh, *Dom!* The baby—I think—I'm losing the baby!'

It was the last thing she could manage, the last coherent thought she had. The next second she had lost herself in a world of fear and dread and total misery and all she knew was that Domenico had reached her. That he was by her side.

Her mind was closing up. She was losing touch with the world, with consciousness and all that mattered was that he was there, big and strong and dependable.

She'd reached home, she knew. She could leave everything up to Domenico now.

And giving up the battle to stay on her feet and fight for consciousness, she collapsed thankfully into the welcoming safety of his arms.

# CHAPTER EIGHT

DOMENICO shifted slightly stiffly in his chair, and stretched limbs cramped with being still for too long. He'd been sitting beside the hospital bed for hours, waiting for Alice to wake up.

And he had no idea what he was going to say to her when she did.

At the moment she lay quiet and peaceful, her eyes closed, long black lashes lying in a luxuriant arc on her colourless skin, her breathing slow and relaxed.

It was all so very different from the moments of horror when she had collapsed in his arms in the bedroom in the early hours of the morning. Then she had been out of her mind in panic, whiter than the hospital sheets, her eyes just unfocused black pools, and her breathing had been so raw and ragged that it had been painful to hear.

He could only be thankful that restless

thoughts, and an even more restless body, had stopped him from sleeping, got him out of bed just as dawn was breaking. He had spent too long lying awake, tossing and turning in a mess of heated bedclothes, not knowing which was worse: closing his eyes and seeing images of Alice's seductive naked body playing out against the screen of his lids—or opening them again and fighting hard against the knowledge that his lover, soon to be his bride, lay in a bed just a short distance away down the corridor and only some feeble English superstition was keeping him from being there with her.

No. Some feeble English superstition and his own sense of unease about this coming wedding.

Because the truth was that from the moment he'd had her agreement to become his wife in the knowledge that her only reasons for giving it had been purely financial, he'd found he just couldn't look at Alice in the same way.

*Only marriage*, she'd said. But it wasn't *only* marriage she had wanted, was it?

He didn't recognise the woman Alice had become. She wasn't the Alice he had first met, the bright, vivacious, delightful girl who had charmed him with her wide smile, her easy confidence. Nor was she the sensual temptress she had become in those first months of living together, her delight in her seductive power over him growing as she gained more confidence in the bedroom.

She wasn't even the Alice who had left him, walked out on their relationship and out of his life because she wasn't having fun any more.

No, in the moment that he had discovered the truth about her pregnancy, she had become something else entirely. Something he had never known before in his life.

Alice and the baby growing inside her were now the family he had never had.

The family he had never had. The family he had told himself he never wanted. The family that was a totally unknown quantity in his life.

'My parents are both dead,' he'd said. 'I have no other relatives.'

And that was the truth—or, rather, the truth as far as he knew it.

The real truth was that he had no idea where his parents were, or even who they had been. Brought up an orphan, in a children's home run by nuns, he had no idea of what having a family might mean, no experience of any such thing.

It had thrown him completely. He had been so knocked off balance that he didn't know what to think, how to react. He didn't know who Alice was, and he didn't know who the hell *he* was.

And so he'd taken several careful steps back, keeping his distance as he tried to assess just how things stood.

'Dom…'

A sigh, the sound of faint movement from the bed brought his eyes back to Alice in a rush.

'Alice? Are you awake?'

She had come round once from the anaesthetic for the operation she had needed this afternoon, but then she had been only half-conscious and not really aware of where she was or what was happening. She had fallen into an exhausted sleep within minutes, and he had been waiting for her to come properly awake ever since.

But no, she had simply stirred in her sleep, coming close to surfacing for a moment and then drifting back into unconsciousness with another sigh.

That sigh twisted something deep inside him

as he reached out a hand to smooth the tangled, tumbled hair away from her forehead, his fingers stroking it down onto the pillow.

'Hush, *cara*,' he soothed, keeping his voice low and soft. 'Sleep now—rest while you can…'

It was better for her that way, Domenico told himself. Better that she should get as much rest as she could, to help her recovery on the way.

There would be sorrow and pain enough for her to face when she did wake.

She didn't know it but there had been times in the past when he had sat and watched her sleeping just as he was doing now, or lain beside her, just staring down into her sleeping face, watching her muscles relax in sleep, seeing the soft curves of her breasts rise and fall with each breath she took. On those occasions he had often had a fierce, determined struggle with himself, the need to lie still and not disturb her warring with the deeper, more primitive need to wake her gently and set himself to seducing her, rousing her body to passionate life beneath his hands and his mouth.

And the more basic need had usually won. He had never been capable of restraint where her luscious body was concerned.

But there were no such thoughts in his head to-day—tonight, he corrected himself, checking his watch and seeing that the trauma of events had swallowed up most of what should have been his wedding day, so that it was now late evening and the point at which he and his new wife should have been about to depart on their honeymoon.

But there would be no honeymoon, just as there had been no wedding—and, most devastating of all, there would be no baby.

*'This child—our baby—is the only other living person in the whole world who has my blood in its veins.'*

His own words came back to haunt him, twisting a knife in his soul.

The baby would have been his only blood relative, his only family, but now there was no baby.

With a rough, jerky movement, Domenico brushed fiercely at his eyes with the back of his hand, dashing away the stinging tears that had blurred his vision. He had never thought about having children—a family—until he'd learned that Alice was pregnant, but over the past two weeks that fact had started to change his world.

But now that change would never happen. And the truth was that he had never known how much he had wanted that child until it was too late.

And what about Alice? How would she react when she realised that the only reason for her agreeing to marry him no longer existed? Would she stay with him or would she see this as the perfect excuse to leave, to find someone new, someone who could give her the sort of life that she had been looking for when she had left him that first time?

'Dom…?'

Another sound from the bed snatched his attention back to where Alice lay, to see that this time she was really waking. Her heavy eyelids fluttered, her head stirred on the pillow and she sighed again.

'Dom?'

'Here,' he said softly, watching as her eyes flew open and went straight to his.

She didn't have to speak a word. Didn't have to ask the question that was so obviously uppermost in her thoughts. It was there, in the darkness of her gaze, in the clouded blue depths of her eyes.

She still had a tiny hope; and he had to be the

one who took it away from her. Reaching for her hand, he closed his fingers around it, knowing that even the small gesture was telling her all she needed to know.

'I'm sorry,' he said huskily.

Alice hadn't needed any words to confirm her worst fears. Deep inside, she had known the truth from the moment that consciousness had started to return to her mind.

The last thing she had really registered was arriving in Domenico's room and seeing him there, tall and strong and dependable, when she most needed him. After that, things had just been one terrible whirl of confusion, horror and pain, and through it all she had held on to Domenico's strength as if it was her only lifeline to reality.

She had heard his voice roaring for help, known that she had been snatched up into his arms and carried out of the room, taking her down into the villa's main hall. The car had been summoned, the chauffeur at the wheel, and Domenico had cradled her close all through the long, fearful journey to the hospital.

At that point she had lost all track of time and place and events. There had been many faces, all unknown, all asking complicated questions in complicated Italian that she couldn't understand.

But once again Domenico had taken charge, answering questions and firing off demands in swift, brusque tones. Weak, in pain and distressed, Alice had simply left everything to him and sunk back inside herself in a desperate attempt to cope. From then on, events had become a terrifying blur in which nothing made sense, until at last the oblivion of unconsciousness had saved her from the worst reality.

She had come round to the silence and the whiteness of the single private room. To soft pillows, crisp, clean sheets and the awareness of the lean, dark, silent figure of Domenico sitting in a chair beside her bed. He had been there every time she had surfaced, opening her eyes just a little, and she had drifted in and out of sleep with a sense of safety and security, knowing he was still there with her, for her.

But there was no hope of staying asleep all the time. She had to wake up and face the truth of what had happened. And if she had had any doubts at all about just what *had* happened then the look in Domenico's eyes, the dark burning gold dulled and clouded, the bruised shadows underneath them, took away any last remaining hope she had.

'I'm sorry,' he said again, his voice gruff and harsh as if coming from a painfully tight throat, and she knew that her baby was gone.

'Oh, no…'

She didn't have the mental strength to lift her head; could only lie there and look into his drawn, shadowed face, seeing her own loss etched there in the lines around his nose and mouth, the tightness of control in the muscles of his jaw.

'Oh, Dom—no.'

The big hand that enclosed hers tightened, squeezing hard as if he wanted to transfer his strength to her.

'Your mother's here—she's just outside. Do you want me to fetch her?'

'No…'

That single word, 'mother', was just too much. It breached all her defences, broke down the barriers she had built up around herself and let the real pain in.

'No,' she managed again. 'I just want you.'

Hot tears flooded her eyes, spilled out down

her cheeks and soaked into the white cotton of the pillow case. She didn't have the strength to hold them back, or even to sob in the way her aching heart needed to express itself, but just let them flow.

'*Porca miseria!*'

As if from a great distance, she heard Domenico mutter fierce imprecations in his native Italian. The next moment he had got up and out of his chair and he was coming down onto the bed beside her, easing her across the mattress gently to make room for his large frame.

'Come here, *cara.*'

His arms came round her, gathered her close, pulled her until she was lying with her head resting against his chest, the soft cotton of his T-shirt beneath her cheek, the heavy thud of his heart in her ear. In the space of only a couple of seconds his shirt was soaked with her tears.

'I'm sorry…' she began, rubbing at her eyes, trying to pull away, but he held her close.

'No,' he said, low, husky and intense. 'No, you need to cry—we both need to mourn. Don't hold back.'

And he held her while the tears poured out of

her and she wept and wept until she had cried herself to a standstill.

'The doctor says you can go home today.'

It was Alice's mother who spoke, her tone that determinedly bright one that she had adopted from the very first moment she had visited her daughter in hospital after her miscarriage.

'That will make you feel so much better, won't it?'

Alice managed a murmur in reply that might have been agreement. She didn't know what to say—and she wasn't at all sure that her mother's description of the Villa d'Acqua as 'home' was at all appropriate.

Domenico hadn't suggested that she go anywhere else. Like her mother, he seemed to have assumed that she was going back to the villa, at least at first, once she left the hospital and needed to recuperate.

But under what circumstances would she be able to live in Domenico's home—and for how long?

She had arrived here less than three weeks before as Domenico's fiancée; the mother of his unborn child. Another day—just a few short hours more—and she would have been his legal wife, with everything signed and sealed, and then the villa would have been her home too. Her home—and that of her child.

Now she had nothing. No baby. No marriage. No home...

And no Domenico?

She didn't know the answer to that question, she admitted as she packed her few belongings into the case her mother had brought with her. Domenico had proposed marriage to her only because she was pregnant. He had changed his mind, moved from his adamant position that he didn't 'do marriage' only because she was pregnant and he was determined that his child should bear his name.

And she had believed that loving both Domenico and his child would be enough to make it worth her while. Now she had no idea if Dom would want her without the baby that had been so important to him. And even if he did, was loving him enough to help her bear a loveless marriage?

A large, wet tear dropped from her cheek onto the nightdress she was laying in the case, leaving a darker, damp patch on the fine silk, and she heard her mother's concerned sigh.

'Oh, darling—don't! It will all come right in the end, you'll see. Give it a few weeks and you'll feel so much better—and then you and Domenico can try again.'

'I don't know if I want to try again, Mum,' Alice admitted. 'I don't want another baby—I wanted this one.'

'Oh, I know—but I don't mean that you should replace the baby you lost. There will always be a place in your heart that is for that baby. But another child to love...'

Another child that would force Domenico into a marriage he didn't want. That would tie him to a marriage with her just to give his baby his name?

'Last time was an accident, Mum,' she said, concentrating fiercely on fastening the case. 'I never meant it to happen. I don't think I want to be a mother after all.'

Something about her mother's silence, a strained quality in the air, made her look up, glancing in the direction of Patricia Howard's face, and then following the direction of the older woman's gaze.

Domenico stood in the doorway. He had appeared, soft-footed and silent, at some point during her conversation with her mother—but she had no idea at just what stage he had actually arrived.

So how much had he heard? It was obvious that he had caught at least part of her last declaration. Alice opened her mouth to take it back, or at least explain, but then, on a hasty second thought, closed it just as quickly again.

It was better this way. Safer. Easier.

If he thought that she never wanted his child in the future, then he wouldn't feel obliged to keep to his offer to marry her. He could be in no doubt that he could have his freedom back. And the man who didn't do marriage would know that she wasn't looking to be his wife in the future.

But if he had heard, he was giving nothing away. His face was closed up, his eyes as unresponsive as the blank stares of marble statues as he came further into the room, reaching out a hand for the case she had just finished packing.

'The car's outside,' he said, his words perfectly even, flat and expressionless. 'Are you ready?'

'Ready as I'll ever be.'

She made it sound as if she really meant it, but the truth was that she was terrified of leaving.

The small blue-painted room with its pristine white sheets and narrow single bed had become like a haven to her over the past few days. A tiny sanctuary where she could hide away from the world, give herself up to her grief at her loss and not have to think about the harsh realities of the outside world.

Now she was going to have to leave the security of her little hideaway and go back into living—and she had no idea at all what the future held for her.

'Come on, then.'

Domenico held out his arm to her and, knowing she had no choice but to do so, she took it and let him lead her out of the door.

# CHAPTER NINE

THE journey back to the villa was as silent, calm and sedate as the desperate journey to the hospital had been frantic, fearful and filled with pain. But for Alice this trip was the time of real desolation. Those words, 'going home', kept repeating inside her head, each time with the dragging sense of dread at the thought that the Villa d'Acqua wasn't home to her at all, and probably never would be now.

She was going back to *Domenico's* home, feeling empty, lost and, in spite of her mother's presence in the car and the fact that her father was waiting for her at the villa, totally alone.

The feeling of loss was almost unbearable.

Alice folded her arms across her body, as if trying to hold herself together, to will her baby to still be there, to make this terrible thing not have happened. But it had, and the misery was compounded by the fact that by losing the baby she had probably lost Domenico too. He had only wanted her as the mother of his child. Now she was no longer that, he couldn't possibly feel the same way.

And that was a thought that was reinforced by the sights that greeted her as they arrived at the villa.

At first she couldn't quite take in what she was seeing. Still numb with shock, it took her bruised mind several lingering seconds to absorb the fact that something was different from the last time she'd been here and process that into a realisation of what had happened—what Domenico had done.

Because only Domenico could have given the order to have all the decorative lights that should have lined the driveway taken down and put away. Only Domenico could have told the gardeners to remove the floral decorations that had been around the huge fountain, flowing over the great stone steps, hanging from the low walls of the terraces.

Only Domenico could have ordered that every trace of their wedding should be removed, erased from existence as if they had never been. Just like the wedding that had never been.

And the wedding that would now never take place?

'We're here,' Domenico announced unnecessarily, bringing the car to a halt at the foot of the steps to the huge main door.

Was the look he turned on her as blank as she read it, or was it just her own battered sensitivity that made it seem so? Was there some hint of question in those brilliant eyes, or was she just imagining everything?

'Are you OK?'

Her hesitation had made him frown.

'I— You had the flowers taken down.'

'I thought it best.'

Now was the time that she had to be strong. She had to hold on to her dignity and face him with a strength she hadn't known she possessed until now. It was time to go back to the pretence she had put on when she had found out about Pippa Marinelli. Time to hide her real feelings behind that mask again.

'Yes,' she said carefully, almost lightly. She even managed a quick, nervous, on-and-off smile. 'I think you're right. It probably is for the best.'

'I'm glad you agree.' Domenico's voice was

unexpectedly gruff. 'Now, can you manage to get up the steps or shall I carry you?'

'I'm all right.'

She'd manage if it killed her. She didn't want to show a moment's weakness, or even response. Domenico's cool indifference on that 'I thought it best' had taken her breath away, and with it all her earlier fears had rushed back with a vengeance.

It was the same once they were inside the house.

All the flowers there had disappeared too. The polished tables, the fine damask cloths, the glittering crystalware might never have been out on display a few short days before. It was as if they had dematerialised, leaving no trace behind.

And she didn't dare to raise a protest, make a comment.

*I thought it best.*

That was what Domenico would say. Cool and flat and adamant. Totally unyielding. It was not something he was prepared to be moved on—or even argue about—and so she might as well not waste her time or deplete the precious little emotional energy that was left to her.

But she couldn't sit and play the loving fiancée to this man, the polite, unconcerned host to her mother and father. She just couldn't do it. She wanted to run and hide, to bury her face in her pillows and pull soft blankets up over her head as she had done in the hospital, and wish the world would go away.

So when Domenico turned to her with that carefully controlled expression on his face, with that social smile that meant nothing at all, and said in a quiet and perfectly pitched tone, 'Would you like something to eat—or a drink?' she simply shook her head, reacting instinctively, defensively.

'I don't need anything—except I'm a little tired. I'd like to lie down.'

'Of course.'

For a moment she was terrified that he would actually suggest coming with her. That he might take her arm to help her up the stairs or, worse, would once again offer to carry her in his arms up to her room. And she just wouldn't be able to bear it.

If he touched her she would break, splintering into a million tiny pieces, and it would be impossible to put her back together again. If Domenico's hand touched hers, or she felt the strength of his arms, the warmth of his body, then she would be lost, remembering what she had once had and what now, it seemed, might have been taken away from her forever.

But something of her thoughts must have shown in her face. Domenico looked into her eyes and read her feelings intuitively and accurately. If he had been about to offer help, then he swallowed the words. He stepped back and away from her, giving her space and leaving the way to the stairs—and to escape— open to her.

'You know where everything is. If you want anything…'

'No! Nothing!'

It was too sharp, too defiant, and it revealed too much. Hastily Alice swallowed down the tension that was twisting her nerves into tight, painful knots. Made herself smile an acknowledgement.

'I'll be fine, thanks,' she managed. 'I just need to rest.'

And before he could say or do anything more, anything that might shatter what little was left of her precarious self-control, she flung herself into climbing up the wide staircase, rushing up the steps as if all the devils in hell were after her and she had to get away from their grasping claws.

She hadn't expected how hard it would be to go into her room. As she put her hand on the door the memories crowded round her, beating at her head and making her hesitate, trembling on the threshold.

The last time she had been here had been on that dreadful night when she had woken in pain and distress and she had fled down the corridor, seeking Domenico and safety. She didn't know if she could make herself go in.

As she stood there she heard quiet footsteps on the polished wooden floor behind her, the sound bringing her head round sharply. Domenico had come up behind her, her small bag in his hand.

'I brought this in case you needed it,' he said, but those narrowed eyes went to her face, took in her hand on the door, her hesitation that told its own story.

'Let me,' he said and, reaching out, he put his fingers over hers, warm and strong, and turned the handle.

He gave the door a little push with his foot

so that it moved, swinging open to give her a clear view of…

But it wasn't her room!

Oh, it was the same *room*—there was the big window giving the wonderful view of the sweeping drive, the big fountain, the glorious gardens, the door to the *en suite* bathroom to her right, the big dressing room to her left…but it was not the room she had left. The place had been totally transformed. The cream and gold decor had vanished, to be replaced with a soft green and white colour scheme, not unlike her bedroom back in the cottage in England. Everything was fresh and crisp and obviously new.

'I had it redecorated,' Domenico said quietly from behind her and, stunned into silence, Alice could only nod blankly, still staring at the scene before her. Taking in the changes that wiped away the links to the terrible memories of that night.

He'd done this for her. He'd known how hard it would be to go into the room, and he'd had it changed so that it was still her bedroom, but it was not the room she had woken up in in the darkest hour of the dawn and known that she was miscarrying.

'Thank you,' she said at last. 'Thank you so much.'

There was no response. Nothing. And suddenly a quality about the silence at her back made her turn sharply, a startled gasp escaping her lips as she realised that there was no one there.

As quietly as he had come, Domenico had disappeared again, moving silently off down the corridor and back down the stairs. Only the case still standing on the floor at her side showed that he had ever been there.

Had he heard her words of thanks? Did he know how much his thoughtfulness in changing the room had meant to her? Alice wasn't sure and for a moment or two she considered going after him to give him her thanks in person, but then, rethinking, she hesitated.

If Domenico had wanted her thanks, he would have stayed around to hear it. Instead he had deposited her case on the floor and gone. He would be back downstairs with her parents again now and he probably wouldn't want her to come rushing down and interrupting things. Besides, the tiredness that she had claimed as an excuse to go to her room had now become a reality. She was still recovering from the physical trauma she'd experienced, and the emotional turmoil that had assailed her since she had left the hospital had reduced her to a limp weariness that meant she only had the energy to head into the room and nowhere else.

Meaning only to dump the case before getting into bed, she headed for the dressing room, freezing in appalled shock as she opened that door and looked inside.

*I thought it best.*

Domenico's voice, controlled, distant, unemotional, came back to her as clearly as if he were standing beside her and speaking the words right in her ear.

*I thought it best.*

Her wedding dress was gone.

Not only her wedding dress but also her shoes, the veil, the delicate headdress. Everything that had been laid out so carefully in the dressing room, ready for her to come and dress herself in them, waiting for the dawn of her wedding day.

The day that had never come.

The day that had never happened and, it seemed,

the day of which Domenico was determined to erase every trace from his life—and hers.

She had coped with the disappearance of the flowers and the lights, the changes downstairs that had removed every sign of the festivities that had been planned but had been so abruptly cancelled. But this…

This careful, deliberate removal of the most personal, most intimate items that had meant her wedding day to her was more than she could bear. It seemed to her that Domenico had set out to obliterate any reminder that there would ever have been a wedding now that in his mind there was no reason for him to marry her after all.

*I thought it best.*

And she had been forced to agree with him. What other choice did she have?

Domenico might not have told her to her face that their marriage was no longer on the cards, but he had found a way to get his message across loud and clear.

In the sunlit garden room downstairs, Domenico finally gave up on his attempt to follow the conversation that Alice's mother and father were having and let his thoughts turn inwards, brooding on the situation in which he found himself.

At some point he knew he was going to have to ask Alice what her thoughts on her future—their future—were. But not now. Not yet.

He had to give her time to heal, to recover from this traumatic loss, before they could look at where they went from here.

Everything had changed so fast. A couple of weeks ago, life had been simple and uncomplicated. Twenty-four hours had changed all that. By the end of one single day he had been anticipating the two major life changes he had thought would never happen to him.

He was going to be a father, and he was getting married.

'I think that would be best. Don't you agree, Domenico?' Patricia asked, turning towards him suddenly.

'Si...' he responded absently, not at all sure what he was agreeing to.

All that he could focus on was just how much like her daughter Patricia Howard was. They had the same deep blue eyes, the same dark, fine hair. Though Patricia's hair was cut into a smooth, elegant style, much shorter than Alice's tumbling mass of waves.

But in another twenty-five years or so, Alice would look much as her mother did now. Smiling, elegant, composed...

Happy?

*Dio mio*, but he hoped so.

'Alice should feel better after she's rested,' Alice's father, David, was saying now. 'Just take things one day at a time. In fact, I think it's probably best if we went home—left you two alone.'

'I agree...'

The rest of Patricia's words faded into an inaudible blur inside Domenico's head. It wasn't the words he was concerned with—it was the smile that she had turned on her husband that caught him and held him transfixed.

It was a smile of agreement and yet it was so much more. It was a smile of trust, of total confidence—the sort of knowledge of a person that could only come from long years of knowing them. Of being together.

And suddenly he had a mental image of Alice, somewhere down the line, twenty, or twenty-five years from now, turning that smile...

On someone else.

*No!*

The rejection of the thought, of the image sounded so violently inside his head that for a moment he was stunned that Patricia and David hadn't heard it. But they continued with their discussion as if nothing had happened—which, to them, it hadn't. And Domenico could only be thankful that they were absorbed in their conversation and didn't seem to notice how he had withdrawn, getting up and pacing to the open French doors and onto the terrace, staring out at the gathering dusk as it crept across the garden.

But he wasn't seeing the expanse of lawn that swept down to the river's edge. He didn't see anything of the vast property he owned and had earned for himself from nothing. From a start with no home, no family, not even a name.

All he could see inside his thoughts was that smile. A smile that told him what it meant to be part of a family. To share a life. To be married.

Two weeks ago his life had changed. Suddenly he was going to be married. And he was going to be a father.

Two weeks ago he'd put those in a different

order. He'd been going to be a father, and so he was getting married.

And now suddenly both of them had been taken away from him. He was no longer going to be a father and…

And marriage?

His thoughts went back to the moment they'd arrived back at the house earlier. The moment that Alice had looked around and noticed the things he'd had done while she was in the hospital. When she'd commented, he'd given her an honest response. 'I thought it best.'

He had thought it was for the best. The reason for their getting married in the first place was gone. Alice had only agreed to marry him because of the baby. Before that— before she'd discovered she was pregnant— she had left him, saying she'd had enough of their relationship.

So with no baby to hold them together, would she stay or would she be glad of the excuse to leave once again and never come back?

He'd thought it best to remove all the signs of the wedding that neither of them had wanted, and Alice had agreed with him.

'I think you're right,' she'd said, as calmly as could be. 'It probably is for the best.'

He'd made the right decision. He was doing what had felt right—and his instincts had been spot on where Alice was concerned. She'd been grateful to see all the evidence of the wedding removed. She'd even managed a smile as a result—the first and only smile since she'd come to him in the greyness of the dawn with a face as white as a sheet and panic darkening her eyes.

She'd smiled. And that smile had told him that she was grateful that he'd anticipated what she wanted and done it without being asked.

Definitely the right thing.

So why the hell did he feel as if he'd just made the worst possible mistake of his life?

# CHAPTER TEN

'YOUR mother and father should be landing about now.'

Domenico made it sound as if his statement was just a casual remark, everyday conversation, but there was still enough of an edge on the words that they made Alice sit up straighter in her chair.

'That's right,' she said carefully, aiming to keep her tone as strictly neutral as his. 'They said it would be at about eight in the evening, our time.'

Now she had to nerve herself for the 'and' or the 'but' that she knew instinctively was coming. She didn't have to wait long.

'Pat said that she asked you to go back with them.'

He didn't lift his eyes from the letter he was reading, keeping them focused on the page, but an unnatural stillness about his posture, a unnec-essary ferocity in his concentration revealed the fact that there was a lot more behind the easy comment than he was letting on.

'Yes—she suggested it might be therapeutic to have a holiday.'

'But you decided not to go?'

'No. Do you think I should have done?'

Oh, this was ridiculous! The two of them were like a pair of hostile cats, nervously circling each other, neither of them daring to look the other straight in the eye for fear that it would spark them into launching a direct attack. So they were both using sidelong glances, oblique approaches, in the hope of suggesting a problem rather than bringing it right out into the open.

And that was 'the problem' right there in that sentence.

Ever since she had come back from the hospital, relations with Domenico had been like this—strained, cautious, careful in the extreme. Nothing was said about the events of the past week, the loss of the baby, and the way it would affect them from now on. Domenico had never, ever raised the topic of what it meant for the future of their relationship—or even if they *had* a relationship that might have a future to follow.

Certainly if she read his behaviour right since she'd come out of hospital, then Domenico had already written off the relationship they'd had and was simply waiting for her to realise it.

'Do you think I should have gone to New Zealand with Mum and Dad?' Alice repeated now, more emphatically. At least if he had to answer that then she might get some clue as to how his mind was working, where his thoughts were heading, so that she might have an idea of how to proceed.

And at least her pointed tone made Domenico pause, lift his head, meet her questioning stare head on.

'Do you?'

Domenico shrugged off the question with a nonchalant lift of one shoulder.

'That depends on what you would like to do. Did you want to go?'

Alice clenched her hand tightly round her water glass until the knuckles showed white.

No! she wanted to scream. No, I do *not* want to go to New Zealand—I don't want to go anywhere! What I want to do is to stay here with you and...

But there her mind blew a fuse. What she wanted

was for time to go back, for things to be as they had been before she had lost her baby. But she knew that that was impossible. It could never be.

The problem was that she had no idea what would happen if she stayed. She only knew that since she had come out of hospital living with Domenico had been like walking on eggshells— and eggshells filled with broken glass, at that!

'I don't think so,' she said cautiously, watching his face intently from between her lashes, waiting to see if some change of expression, some reaction, however small, would give her a clue as to what he was thinking or feeling.

But there was none. Just as there had been no reaction, no show of any emotion, to anything all week. He had been politeness and courtesy itself. If there was anything she wanted, needed or even just had a passing whim for, then it was hers. But what she wanted was some sign of Domenico himself. The real man behind the unrevealing mask which was all he was showing her.

And that she was not allowed to see.

'Then you're better staying here,' Domenico returned calmly, dropping his gaze back to the letter in his hand.

'You don't mind?'

'Why should I mind? There's plenty of room and if you don't feel up to travelling…'

'It isn't the travelling that bothers me!'

His indifference stung. If he had made up his mind about their future, then he was not saying. If he had any thoughts at all about where they went from here then he clearly had no plans to share them with her.

'I just think Mum and Dad need time to themselves without me around. After all, they're almost newly-weds in a way.'

That got his attention. He actually put the letter aside as his eyes went to her face, a faint frown of confusion drawing his brows together.

'How can they be newly-weds? They must have been together—what, twenty-six years?'

'Because I'm twenty-five? Well, yes, they were together twenty-six years ago, but they haven't always been together in between.'

'They split up?'

'About eight years ago. They were rowing all the time and they decided on a separation. They'd even put the divorce in motion. That was when Mum moved to New Zealand—she has a sister out there. But one day Dad's company sent him out to Auckland to complete a deal. On an impulse, he decided to look up Mum. They had a meal together—and another… In the end they realised they didn't want to divorce at all. So they cancelled the whole thing.'

'And your father moved out to New Zealand too?'

Alice nodded, a faint smile curving her mouth.

'They felt they needed a new start—and that New Zealand had been lucky for them, so they wanted to stay there. That's why I said they're only like newly-weds really. They've just bought a new house and are enjoying rediscovering each other. I'm so happy for them and I wouldn't want to…'

Her voice caught in her throat as her gaze tangled with his and she caught the expression in the darkness of his eyes, snagging on something raw and unshielded that was hidden there.

'How does it feel?' he said suddenly and for a moment she couldn't understand what he was asking, or even why he had come out with the question.

'How…?'

'How does it feel to be able to talk like that?

To know about your parents; who they are, where they live—what they did in the past?'

'It…'

Alice found she couldn't answer him. To her, it just felt normal. Perfectly ordinary. She couldn't begin to think what it would feel like *not* to know.

'Did you never know your parents?'

'Never.'

'Oh, Dom! I can't imagine what that feels like. For me, Mum and Dad have always been there. Even when they split up they were there for me. They're part of my life and always have been. They're what helps me define myself. And of course my past—my memories—are full of them.'

'I have no memories.'

'None at all?'

Everything in her was pushing her to get out of her chair, go over to him, take his hand…but one look at his dark, controlled face warned that her actions would not be welcome.

'You—you must have been very young when they died.'

'I was *neonato*—newborn.'

It was the sheer matter-of-factness of the statement that caught on Alice's heart and twisted. He showed no emotion, no sense of horror, while even to imagine anything happening to either of her parents, never mind both, brought the hot sting of tears to her eyes.

But then, of course, Domenico had been too young to register his parents, too young to remember anything about them.

'What—?' she began, but Domenico either wasn't listening or was determined to cut her off before she probed any deeper.

'That's why I'm not exactly used to having someone's parents around the house.'

Was he saying that was also why he had been so distant and impenetrable for the past few days? That it was because of her parents and not because their relationship was over as far as he was concerned? Or was it that he hadn't felt right at the thought of finishing things with her while her parents were here?

'Is that why you kept your distance while Mum and Dad were here?'

She meant it to sound joking but it somehow got mangled up between her thoughts and her tongue and came out as provocative instead.

'You needn't have worried—they're no prudes.

They would expect us—as an engaged couple—to share a bed.'

The sensation of having put her foot squarely in her mouth hit home with a sickening sense of horror uncoiling in the pit of her stomach.

Engaged.

*Were* they engaged?

He had proposed marriage because she was pregnant with his child, and only because she was pregnant. So did he still consider his offer binding now that she had lost the baby?

She opened her mouth to ask but lost her nerve and found herself saying instead, 'Did you really think that they'd play the heavy parents because—?'

'That is a very stupid question,' Domenico inserted with a razor-sharp edge to the words. 'Do you really think that I'm crass enough to force myself on you when you've just been through such a trauma?'

And did she really think that he had forgotten it already? That he could just switch off from the memories of just over a week ago? Hell, if he closed his eyes now, he could still see her the way she'd been when she'd burst into his room, with her eyes wide and staring in shock, her face whiter than the nightdress she was wearing, the spots of blood on the silky material that had told their own story of horror and loss.

'I do have some sense of control, even if you might find it hard to believe.'

He wished he'd moderated his tone better when he saw her flinch, but she'd caught him on the raw. For the past few days she'd drifted through his life like a pale, withdrawn wraith. She would neither talk about the miscarriage nor let him get anywhere near her. She had seemed as hard to get close to, get hold of, as a rainbow or a drift of snow in the wind.

And now *she* was accusing *him* of keeping his distance!

'So it's just "control", is it?' Alice challenged, suddenly more animated than she'd been in days. Her head had come up, tossing back the cloud of dark hair that tumbled round her face, and her big eyes had a flash of life in them that had been missing ever since she'd woken up in the hospital. Nothing else?'

'And what does that mean?'

'Exactly what I said. That it's only a "sense of

control" that's keeping you in your room and not in mine?'

'That's what I said.'

'Yes, I know that's what you said, but is that the truth? Are you sure that there's nothing else that might be causing the problem?'

'What else would there be?'

Tossing the letter down onto the table, Domenico raked both hands through his hair as he tried to follow her abrupt changes of mood, struggling to see any logic behind them. He believed he had behaved like a gentleman, but it seemed that in her mind she was accusing him of something else entirely.

'Alice—this is—'

'Stupid! Yes, I know!' she interrupted, her voice so brittle that he expected the words to splinter into tiny pieces on the carpet in front of him. 'I know—it's stupid—'

Flinging herself to her feet, she paced restlessly about the room, hands shoved into the side-pockets of her deep pink dress, the flowing skirt swirling about her legs with each brusque, jagged movement.

'I'm stupid!'

'Damn it, Alice!'

Disbelief, annoyance and a great wave of exasperation swept through him, pushing him out of his chair and across the room towards her. Grabbing hold of her arms, he pulled her to a halt, the force of the action swinging her round to face him. She was paler than ever, but this time it was the pallor of suppressed emotion, her eyes clashing violently with his, her expression radiating defiance and rejection.

'Just when did I say you were stupid? I never said any such thing and you know I didn't! Just what is going through that muddled head of yours that makes you think such crazy thoughts?'

'First stupid—now crazy, huh?'

Alice's face was sending him completely contradictory messages to her voice. Her words were cold and sharp, impossibly harsh, while her facial expression was a blend of defiance and distress, her chin tilted challengingly, her blue eyes sheened with tears. But were they tears of anger or unhappiness? He couldn't judge, and, given the volatile mood she was in, she would probably go up in flames if he even asked.

Clearly he was supposed to know just what

was going on in her mind, without being given so much as a clue.

'I'm surprised that you want to waste your time with a mad woman like me—that you'll even give me houseroom.'

'Give you—' Domenico began, but Alice's tongue was running away with her and she cut straight across him without even listening to what he was saying.

'But then, of course, it wouldn't do to show me the door when my parents were here, now, would it? I mean that would be really "crass" and of course you don't do crass just as you don't do—' Abruptly she swallowed down whatever she had been about to say. 'As you don't do loss of control!'

'So now my restraint is being held against me, is that it?'

Domenico could feel his grip on the reins of his temper sliding away from him. He was beyond knowing which way she was going to jump next. And his attempts at guessing what she wanted from him were exploding right in his face. It seemed that he was expected to know without any clues and then get shot down anyway, no matter what happened.

'I'm trying to be considerate here, Alice, but you're not making it easy!'

'Considerate!'

Alice wrenched herself away from his grip, whirling round and flouncing off across the room. When the barrier of the wall blocked her way, she swung back again to face him, hands on hips, eyes flashing, mouth set.

'So you're trying to be *considerate,* are you, Dom? *Considerate!* So tell me—what's considerate about the way you behaved when you brought me back here? When I'd just got out of hospital?'

'You're going to have to explain that accusation.' Domenico's fight to keep his temper damped down turned his voice into a cold snarl, made his words snap out like the toughest commands. 'Because it seems to me that I'm being tried and condemned before I even know what I'm charged with! It's obvious that you think I'm guilty, but of what?'

'You don't know?'

The look she flung in his direction was openly sceptical, taking any remaining warmth from her face and turning it into the face of an ice maiden, bloodless, frozen and totally remote. She was completely armoured against him, shields up to repel any advances, and she had no intention of letting anyone get past any of her defences.

'Obviously I don't know or I wouldn't be asking! Alice…at least sit down and let's discuss this rationally.'

'I don't want to sit down!'

Her hands came up before her face in a wild, defensive motion that also had the effect of cutting off all communication between them, breaking even the delicate strands of eye contact.

'And I don't want to do as you tell me—and I most definitely do not feel rational about this! But I'll just bet that you felt totally rational—and so much in control when you—'

'When I what?'

Domenico's control cracked and he couldn't hold back the roar of frustration; couldn't disguise the exasperation that was chafing at him, fraying his ability to keep his irritation in check.

He had thought he'd been prepared for anything that might result as an after-effect of the miscarriage. Depression, withdrawal—he'd expected those. Tetchiness and a volatile mixture of emotions…those too. But this was something else. This cold-eyed, cold-voiced woman with the colourless face and the ice-blue eyes was an Alice he had never encountered before. A chilly, hissing harridan who clearly loathed him.

'If you're going to start treating me as the devil incarnate, or as some sort of beast from the primeval swamps, then at least do me the courtesy of explaining *why*. Even a serial killer gets a chance to defend himself! To answer the crimes he's accused of!'

'Crimes!'

It came on a cynical laugh, one that he doubted he'd ever heard from Alice before. And it didn't sound at all right coming from her soft mouth while scepticism shadowed her beautiful eyes. If he'd thought earlier that her appearance was at odds with her voice, then it was happening again. But this time it was impossible to believe that such bitterness, such black sarcasm could come from someone as delicately beautiful as the woman before him.

It might be fury that sparked in her eyes, but it gave them a glow like the most beautiful, most polished sapphires he had ever seen. And even though cynicism and accusation were what came from her mouth, they were still the most sensual, most kissable lips he had ever seen. And if she tossed her proud head once more, flinging back the shining dark mane of hair and stamping her foot like the proudest, most glorious, thoroughbred Arab mare, then he was going to lose all control.

He just wanted to stride forward and grab her. To slide his hands into that fall of hair and twist it around his fingers, holding her tight. He wanted to turn that proud head towards his and take the softness of her mouth under his, kissing her until she was lost in sensation, until those angry blue eyes shut and she softened under his caress, forgetting all the wild accusations in the moment of yielding up to him, moving instantly from the fierce arousal of fury to the softer but no less potent excitement of pleasure.

But as he took a single step forward, she edged away again, nervous as a wary cat, the look in her eyes warning that if he tried that again then she would run.

And so he forced himself to stay where he was. Forced his mouth to speak softly, to control the urge to lash out, match her accusations with some of his own, parry the slashing attacks of her tongue with a ferocity that matched and out-stripped her rage.

'Yes—if you're going to start throwing accu-sations around then at least tell me the crimes I've committed.'

'Do I have to spell it out? Oh, but I see that I do, because you don't even care what you've done—you don't even *see* it.'

'*Porca miseria!* I don't know what the devil I'm supposed to see!'

'Well, what about the sight that greeted me when I came ho—when I got back here from the hospital? What about the way that all the flowers had vanished—all the lights? All the decorations and the candles?'

'I thought—'

But Alice rushed on.

'What about the way that every trace of our wedding had disappeared—the cake, the mar-quee—even…'?

Her voice broke on a sob that stopped her speech for a moment. Once again Domenico tried to take a step forward but a furious hand came up to wave him away.

'Even my wedding dress? Do you know how I felt when I looked in that room and my dress had gone? And you call that considerate?'

'Yes, I do, damn you! I do!'

'Then what the blazes are you like when you're being inconsiderate? Because if this is your *consideration,* then I'd sure as hell hate to be around when you're being *mean!*'

'Oh, I can be mean if you want me to, Alice.' Domenico's tone had smoothed to a silken purr, a purr that was soft as a tiger's paw—with lethal, cruel claws concealed just out of sight. 'But I swear you wouldn't like it. And I wasn't being cruel when I—'

'No, of course not!' Alice spat at him, blue eyes flashing fire. 'Of course not! You just—'

She broke off in shock as Domenico flung up his arms in exasperation.

'I thought you wouldn't want reminding of the wedding that your pregnancy had forced you into! I thought that you already had enough on your plate without worrying about a promise that you'd made under duress. I thought—'

'You thought it best!'

'Yes!'

'You thought it *best*—and you thought of everything! Well, no, not everything…'

Her left hand came up, fingers spread. With her right one she was tugging at something on the third finger.

The ring. The engagement ring that he had insisted on buying when she had agreed to marry him. The ring he had chosen with such care, because she had given him something he had never thought he would have—the chance of a family of his own.

'That—' he began but had to leave the sentence hanging when she flung the ring at him with such force that he had to turn his face aside swiftly to avoid being hit on the cheek.

'There was no need—' he tried again.

'There was every need!' she cut across him, tossing her hair back as she faced him with challenge and defiance stamped into every inch of her. 'Because now you have everything! Every damn thing that would ever remind me of that unwanted wedding! You have everything—and I'm free!'

Well, that told him, Domenico reflected cynically. Now he knew exactly where he stood;

exactly what she thought of his proposal, of the thought of ever being married to him.

And he could only be thankful that he'd never opened his stupid mouth and let her in on his thoughts—the momentary dream—of the night that he had brought her home from the hospital. Now, as then, silence was clearly the best policy.

'Yes,' he said stiffly, 'you're free to do whatever you want.'

'Well, in that case, I'm sure you won't mind if I pack! I can be out of here in an hour and then you'll never have to see me again!'

He meant to let her go. He really did. It was so obvious that all she wanted was to get out of here—and fast—that he knew he would just be wasting his time even attempting to dissuade her.

He even stood back to allow her space to get past him, a free path to the door.

And he clamped his mouth shut, pushed his hands deep into his pockets, to armour himself against any weak and foolish attempt to hold her back.

He was fine while she was still; while she was standing there, glaring at him, her slender body stiff and taut with rejection, her eyes blue chips of ice. But something happened as she came past him.

Perhaps it was the brush of the skirt of her dress against his body. Perhaps it was the waft of her perfume on the air, the scent of her skin that seemed to reach out with delicate, sensitive fingers and coil around him, chaining him to her with strands so fine and yet so strong that he knew he would never be free.

Or maybe it was the flash of something in her eyes as, just for a second, she turned her head and looked straight into his face. Something that clashed with his own gaze, then snagged and caught—and held it...

'No!' he said, the word breaking from him, impossible to hold back. 'No!'

And, wrenching his hands from his pockets, he reached out and grabbed at her arm, hauling her to a halt and holding her there.

# CHAPTER ELEVEN

'No?'

Alice couldn't believe what she had heard.

It wasn't possible.

And yet it was such a simple word, one that barely sounded like anything else. So what else could it be? What else could it mean?

And there was that hand on her arm, strong fingers curled around it, just above her elbow. What else could it mean, when combined with that single syllable but…?

'No?' she repeated, searching his face for clues and finding none.

'Don't go.' Domenico spoke with husky ferocity. 'I don't want you to go.'

Her heart jerked violently in her chest. Was this real? Had he actually said…?

'Wh-what did you say?'

'I said don't go.'

'Why?' she croaked, forcing the word past lips that were painfully dry and tight even though she had slicked them with a moist pink tongue just seconds before.

'Why?' Domenico echoed on a questioning note and there was a small smile that curled his lips as if he couldn't believe that she had even had to ask. 'Does this give you a clue?'

And he slid his free hand under her chin, holding her face up to his as he bent his head and closed his lips over hers.

Alice had never known a kiss like it. It was long and slow and drugging in its sensuality, but at the same time it had a fierce intensity that made her head spin. It was searching, demanding, infinitely hungry and yet it also enticed and cajoled, seeming to draw her heart out of her body and have her soul follow it.

His tongue slid across her mouth, marking the line where her lips had parted, not intruding, not invading, but gently inviting her to open up to him. And Alice could do nothing but respond, her lips parting on a gasp of delight and surrender, her mouth opening, her own tongue enticing him in.

Domenico made a low, raw sound deep in his throat and gathered her close to him, one arm coming round her, to pull her up against his body, the other sliding into her hair, tangling in the dark strands, hard fingers splaying against the curving bone of her skull. Gently but irresistibly, he turned her to him, angling her head just so that he could kiss her again, harder this time, taking her mouth on a long, slow, sensual journey that burned his brand on her lips, turned her blood molten in her veins and set her senses zinging with electricity all over her body.

'Get the idea?' he muttered against her mouth. And Alice could only sigh a wordless sound of agreement and acquiescence as her lips sought his again, needing the hot pressure even after that tiny space of snatched speech that had stopped him kissing her.

Her own hands had gone up and around his neck, pulling his head down to hers, as she stood on tiptoe to press herself closer, giving back every bit as much as he had given her, and adding something more. The heat from his body against which she was pressed seemed to sear her from top to toe, burning through the fine material of her dress and scorching the wakened flesh beneath.

But it wasn't enough. It could never be enough. Not when what she truly wanted was his hands on her, the burn of his palms on her skin, the hardness and strength of his fingers caressing the most delicate points on her body. The heavy pulse of need low down in her body set every nerve throbbing in aching hunger.

She had thought that she was being dismissed, that he wanted no more of her, and this sudden about-turn made her head swim. She felt as if she had been starving and now she was finally being offered something. It wasn't enough to appease her aching hunger, and it probably wouldn't sustain her for more than a very short space of time, but she was so, so hungry that she knew she was going to grab at it with both hands before it evaporated totally.

'So you do still want me—want me here?'

'Want you?' Domenico's laughter was raw-edged, catching in his throat as he vented it. 'Oh, *cara*, do you have to ask?'

Did she need to ask? Well, no, not really. The heavy pounding of his blood that built a pulse at the base of his throat, the heat that radiated from his skin, the ragged, uneven breathing all told their own story. She had known and loved this man so long that she was attuned to every tiny sign that revealed how aroused he was, and she couldn't doubt them now.

She knew that he *wanted* her, and that was enough for him. But was it enough for her?

Was she really so desperate that she would take whatever crumbs he would toss her and accept them gratefully, as being just enough to stop her from starving without ever actually nourishing any part of her?

But then Domenico's mouth touched her ear, his lips warm and his tongue moistly tracing the contours of the skin, his teeth faintly grazing the curving outer edge, and everything inside her melted in the rush of heat along every nerve path. The tips of her breasts stung where they were crushed against the hard wall of his chest, her lower body moved sinuously against his, bringing a low groan to his mouth as she slid against the swelling force of his arousal, feeling its heat even through their clothes.

His dark head came down to kiss her again, his

mouth crushing hers, his tongue invading, stroking intimately over the soft inner tissues so that she shivered in excitement.

The hand that had held her had loosened and was stroking slowly, softly down the bare skin of her arm. Tantalising caresses circled over her hand, moving down each finger in turn before he caught her palm in his and lifted it to the warm pressure of his mouth. This time it was his lips that kissed their way down each finger, lingering over the spot where her engagement ring had been and enclosing the now empty space in a warmth that seemed to ease the sense of loss. And all the time he was muttering soft words in her ear, husky, caressing, cajoling words in liquid Italian that made her heart melt as she caught at their meaning. She spoke enough of the language to recognise the ardent praise of her beauty, the declarations of adoration, the need, the hunger that was driving him wild, making him crazy.

And her own mouth moved almost silently, echoing and repeating the phrases to him, pressing the words against his skin in slow, tender kisses on the lean planes of his cheek. The rough growth of beard abraded her lips and she let the tip of her tongue slide out to touch the warmth of his skin. The clean, faintly salty taste of his flesh and the heady, male scent rushed to her head like a potent wine, intoxicating and stimulating. She felt drunk in seconds—drunk on pleasure—and the small, provocative taste was just not enough.

'Dom!'

With a small, whimpering moan, she sought his mouth again, becoming braver now, more demanding, pressing her lips to his, letting her own tongue mimic his explorations earlier, and smiled inwardly as she felt his instant response. The stroke of his hands over her body became harder, hungrier, more urgent. His caresses found the swell of her breasts, cupping and enclosing each one in a searing heat so that she writhed in uncontrolled response, pressing her needy body closer into his hands, hungry nipples peaking against the warmth of his palms.

'Alicia—*carissima*…'

With a gasp he wrenched his mouth away to snatch in a much-needed breath, his broad chest heaving. Looking down into her face, his molten bronze eyes met the yearning blue of hers and he reached up a noticeably unsteady hand to push it through her hair once more, holding her head just so—tilted up to him. Their gazes locked, unable to look away.

'Come with me, *mi fidanzata,*' he muttered in a voice that was thickened with passion. 'Come upstairs with me and let me show you that I want you—let me show you how much I want you here, with me…'

*Mi fidanzata.*

*My fiancée.*

Alice's already whirling brain could only fasten on that one word and the important meaning it had—the way that Domenico had used it when he could have said so many others.

*Mi fidanzata.*

Just two small words but they were enough.

'Come with me now,' Domenico said again, and she looked up into those burning eyes, seeing the way that the pupils had expanded, huge and dark with just a circle of glowing gold around the rim. She couldn't speak, though her mouth opened to try, but she didn't need to because something in her face had given her away.

And Domenico had caught it. She saw his eyes

narrow, saw him register the silent answer she had given him with a quick, decisive nod. The next moment he had crushed another hard, fierce kiss on her parted lips before catching her up in his arms, lifting her and carrying her towards the sweeping stairs.

Instinctively Alice's arms went around his neck, though she knew she was held safely, with his strength supporting her. Her eyes were still locked with his so she barely saw their progress up the polished wood, or even registered just where they were on their journey to the wide expanse of the landing. She only knew the feel of the wall against her back as, every couple of steps or so, he paused to kiss her again, turning their progress into a form of foreplay that inflamed her senses and heated her blood.

By the time they reached the landing, she was gasping with need and had already tugged loose the top four buttons on his shirt that were all she could reach. But it was enough to reveal the powerful straight lines of his shoulders, the pulse that beat at the base of his neck, against which she pressed her hungry mouth, licking, sucking and nibbling the exposed skin, feeling his pulse kick up a beat under her caresses, his raw groan of response a husky sound low in his throat.

As he lowered her to her feet he let her body slide down the length of his, chest to chest, thigh to thigh, the slenderness of her hips cradled in the strong bones of his pelvis. By the time she was standing on her own feet, her legs were trembling almost too much to support her as a result of the onslaught on her senses and her knees threatened to buckle beneath her.

But Domenico didn't intend that she should stay there long. As soon as he had a hand free he found the long zip that fastened her dress at the back and slid it swiftly down. A heartbeat or two later the whole dress slithered down her body, falling to the floor to pool in a swirl of pink linen on the deep blue carpet.

Deep blue.

It was only then that Alice registered just where she was. That Domenico had brought her up and into *his* room, not hers. That fact seemed significant, but for the life of her she couldn't quite put her finger on why. And her whirling brain's scrabble to find an explanation spun off into oblivion as Domenico kissed her again and slid her unfastened bra from her aching breasts, dropping it to the floor to lie, pale pink against dark, on top of her crumpled dress.

*'Alicia, cara...'*

Her name was a crooning litany against her skin as he swept her up again, carried her to the bed and came down beside her.

*'Carina, adorata, tesora...'*

With gentle hands he shaped her body, lingering at the curves of breasts and hips, his eyes hooding and a smile curving his mouth as he watched her writhe underneath his touch, her yearning body arching upwards, pressing herself against him.

'Dom...'

The affectionate form of his name escaped her on a cry of need as his touch tormented the aching tips of her breasts, tugging lightly on the tightened nipples.

'Dom...please...'

Experience of loving her in the past told him just what she wanted and he bent his proud head to take one of the rosy pink tips in his mouth, swirling his tongue around and over it, bringing it to burning, stinging life before closing his lips over it and suckling hard.

And as it had always been in the past, that was the point at which her fraying hold on her control broke. Her head flung back against the pillows, her body arcing into his, as her impatient fingers completed the task of unfastening and removing his shirt that she had begun on the journey upstairs.

Domenico helped her, shrugging his broad shoulders out of the garment and tossing it to the floor. His trousers followed, and then the black trunks that Alice had been pushing at impatiently, desperate to have the whole man as naked as she was, the whole muscular length of his hot, satin flesh covering hers.

For as long as it took to draw in a breath or two that satisfied them, but no longer. As soon as Alice's wandering hands found their way down the long, straight line of his back and smoothed the tight curve of his buttocks, Domenico moved convulsively, jerking in response to her caress. And that abrupt movement brought the heated power of his erection into burning contact with the nest of dark curls at the juncture of her thighs.

Immediately her fingers slid between their

bodies, touching softly, smoothing over the heated velvet that sheathed the masculine force of him, making him buck in uncontrolled reaction, his own hands tightening in the dark cloud of hair spread out around her head.

'Careful,' he muttered, thick and raw. 'Don't... Alice—*don't!*—*Momento*...'

In a frantic movement he pulled away, twisting on the bed and reaching for the small cabinet that stood beside it. Wrenching open a drawer, he pulled out a small foil packet and ripped it open.

Alice had barely time to register what was happening before he had sheathed himself and was once more lying with her, the hair-hazed strength of one leg coming between hers, nudging her thighs aside, sliding between them.

Cupping her head in both his hands, he looked down deep into her face, his glittering eyes searching her passion-scorched features. His black hair had fallen forward over his broad forehead and high on the carved cheekbones a raw slash of colour burned his skin.

Bending to touch her lips, he took them once in a long, drugging kiss before lifting his head just inches so that his nose was against hers and the breath from his mouth was warm on her cheek.

'Now,' he muttered roughly as the tip of his masculinity probed the moist core of her. 'Now I will show you how much I want you. And why I want you here…with me…'

With each phrase he thrust himself into her, a little further and a little harder every time, making her hungry body clench around him, a moan of response escaping her lips.

Domenico moved again. In…and almost out…and in again.

As his thrusts picked up strength and speed, Alice moaned, her head tossing on the pillow, long dark hair flying over her face, catching on her lips. Domenico kissed it aside, took her mouth for his own.

With his hands on her body too, she was lost in a world of sensation, swimming in it, drowning in it, going down under swirling waves of pleasure. Giving her whole self up to it, she closed her eyes tight, concentrating fiercely on the glorious pressure building up and up, deep inside her. But even as she felt it grow, knew where it was heading, Domenico moved again, shifting his lips to take one pouting nipple hard into his mouth and suckling on it hard.

Immediately Alice's control shattered, taking any form of rational or coherent thought with it. Losing herself completely, she arced her body upwards, giving herself totally to this man, taking him totally into herself. A wild, keening cry of stunned delight broke from her as the pleasure flooded through her, taking all defences, all restraint along with it. Somewhere in the back of what tiny fragment of her mind was still functioning, she was instinctively aware of the fact that Domenico too had reached the same peak at the same time, as a hoarse cry of fulfilment was torn from him, his long body tensing, his dark head thrown back as her heated innermost core convulsed around him. But that was the last thing she knew as the next moment the stormy waves of orgasm broke inside her body, swarmed through every nerve, crashed over her head, and took her whirling and spinning and sobbing out loud into the blind oblivion of ecstasy.

# CHAPTER TWELVE

THE MUTED buzzing of his mobile phone, some-where in the room, was the last thing on earth that Domenico wanted to hear.

He didn't want to know about the outside world, didn't want to *think* about anything else but what he had here, in this space, in the heat and comfort of this bed, with this woman at his side, her glorious female body limp and exhausted, satiated as he was by the fiery passion that had consumed them both.

Satiated? Well, temporarily.

His heart was still slowing from the frantic, urgent racing of fulfilment. His breathing had eased, returning to normal from the raw rasp of sexual ecstasy, and the sheen of sweat had evap-orated from his body. Already his recovery was close to complete.

In his mind he was already there, already anticipating the point when, with the afterglow of gratification ebbing away at last, and the nagging tug of need driving away the lazy contentment of this moment, he would reach for Alice once more. He would kiss the softness of her yielding, giving lips, savour the intimate, uniquely personal taste of her mouth, bury his tongue in its moist, welcoming warmth. His hands would explore the silken contours of her body, tracing paths they'd been before, finding pleasure spots he knew from a lover's experience always drove her wild. Maybe he'd find some that even he had yet to discover, the hidden secrets of her beauty that would take him a lifetime to fully enjoy, to truly apprcciatc. His touch would arouse his own hunger with each kiss and each caress, awakening a matching desire in her, nurturing the still-glowing embers of their passion until they flared once more into the wild and unstoppable fire of need that would consume them both in its demanding force.

It was a prospect that he anticipated with the deepest pleasure. Even now, just thinking about it, he felt his body already growing hard and hot, his senses starting to rediscover the anticipation and primitive excitement that he knew would soon build to a brutal demand for fulfilment if he denied them too long.

But the persistent electronic buzzing of his phone forced itself into his consciousness, driving through the clinging cobwebs of his lethargy and demanding his attention *now*, before it woke Alice too, and turned her mind to more practical and mundane matters than the sensual feast he had been anticipating. Already she was beginning to stir and mutter faintly, a small frown creasing the smooth space between her fine, dark brows.

*'Porca miseria!'* Domenico swore under his breath as, flinging back the bedclothes, he forced his unwilling body out of the bed, swinging his legs to the floor and standing up reluctantly.

Where the devil was the damn thing? Why hadn't he left it in his jacket pocket as he usually did? Then it would still be downstairs and the unwelcome caller wouldn't have intruded on the sensual idyll that he had been enjoying.

The idyll he had every intention of prolonging right through the night. He had every intention of making love to Alice again and again, over and over, in every way he could imagine and some he had yet to dream up—but ones he was sure that the combination of her luscious sensuality and his erotic imagination could invent for their drawn-out delight.

'Go away!'

Mentally he cursed the caller's persistence, wishing on them a battery failure, a power cut, the loss of credit—anything just so that they would go away and leave him alone to….

But then he realised what time it was; recalled just who he had asked to ring him at this hour, why he had told her to use the mobile and not the main house phone, and what her call might mean. Immediately the slow reluctance of lethargy dropped from him and he moved quickly to where the tangled bundle of his clothes lay abandoned on the carpet. Snatching up the crumpled trousers, he tugged the slim, silver-coloured phone from their pocket and thumbed it on.

'*Si?*'

The voice that answered him in Italian was the female one he had been expecting; the one that made it awkward and impossible to take the

phone call where he was. He couldn't talk freely
and, besides, in the bed Alice was stirring again,
her tousled head turning on the pillow, her long,
smooth limbs stretching and relaxing as she
drifted closer to wakefulness.

'I'll ring you back,' he said softly, hastily
switching off the phone again and gathering up
the rest of his clothes in one hand as he moved
swiftly to Alice's side of the bed and knelt down
on the rich blue carpet at her side, gently stroking
the tangled dark hair away from her face with the
hand that still held the phone.

'*Cara...*'

It was low-voiced, soothing, stilling her
restless movement, making her smile in recog-
nition of his voice.

Smiling too, in unseen response, and unable to
resist it, he bent his head and took her mouth in
a lingering kiss, then cursed inwardly as the
intimate caress created a savage kick of primal
need low down in his body. A need that he knew
he was going to have to deny himself the
pleasure of indulging—for a little while at least.

'Dom...'

His name was a sleepy sound of pleasure on

Alice's tongue, twisting his physical and mental discomfort several notches higher as she stirred languorously and reached out sleepy arms to fold around his neck. The dreamy smile on her soft pink lips was almost irresistible, but Domenico knew that if he gave in to temptation then the next phone call that interrupted them would be impossible to conceal. Alice would want to know who it was from and he could not lie to her.

And there would be another phone call—and soon, he knew. Pippa Marinelli was not a patient woman, and she wouldn't take kindly to being kept waiting.

'I have to take this, *cara,*' he said, kissing her closed eyelids instead.

He wanted her to keep them closed; was not at all sure that if she woke up properly, opened her eyes, she might not read something in his face that would make her want to enquire further into the reason for his leaving her right now. She might even guess at the identity of the caller, and they had too much to talk about as it was.

'I'll answer it downstairs. I know...' he murmured ruefully, anticipating her frown of displeasure, the small pout of her lips. 'I know, and I don't want to, either. But I won't be long. And now that you're staying we have all the time in the world.'

His smile grew, became a wide, reminiscent grin, even though he knew that she couldn't see it.

'I knew I could make you stay. Knew you'd see we're not ready to be apart—not now...'

Not ever? his unguarded mind added in the privacy of his own thoughts. But that was another subject he could only raise when they had enough time—more time than was available to him now.

'Sleep now.'

'But...'

Once again her mouth formed that sexy little moue of protest, threatening both his composure and his resolve. But each movement of his left hand brought the sleek lines of his cellphone back into the range of his vision, reminding him that he didn't have the time to indulge the yearning demands of his senses,

'You need to rest, *cara*,' he insisted. 'And I'll be back by the time you wake. Wait here for me and we'll take up where we left off. I'll tell you when you can get up.'

And that was as much delay as he dared risk, so he gently but firmly eased himself from her entwining arms, tucking them down at her sides and pulling the bedclothes up around her, hiding the provocative temptation of her naked body from his hungry gaze. He couldn't resist one last snatched moment to press a lingering kiss on the rounded curve of her shoulder, almost groaning aloud as she murmured softly, the faint, warm sound of sensual contentment twisting nerves already tight with the struggle to resist.

'Come back soon,' she murmured, nestling down deeper into the pillows and sighing reluctantly.

'Oh, I will,' he promised, huskily fervent. 'As soon as I can.'

And then, because it was either leave *now*—and fast—or abandon all attempts to go and give in to the need that was driving him half-insane, he forced himself to his feet, and out of the door.

He was more than halfway down the landing, almost at the top of the stairs, before he felt ready enough to stop, draw in a deep, ragged breath and bring himself under the control needed to pull on his clothes and restore himself to some degree of normality.

The phone he still left switched off, however. Out of sight of Alice's feminine temptations, he was at last beginning to think rationally again. He was not prepared to take any risks, he told himself as he ran down the stairs and headed for his office. There was still the possibility that Alice might awaken and come after him. He wanted to have this conversation in complete privacy before he decided whether he was prepared to share the contents of it with anyone or not.

In the privacy of his study he shut the door carefully. Then pulled the phone out of his pocket again and thumbed it on.

'Pippa? What have you got to tell me?'

At first, Alice was quite content to lie where she was and wait for Domenico to come back. She was warm and comfortable and very relaxed, and so indolently satisfied that for a while she was not even remotely inclined to move. It was just so easy to lie there, and doze, and think of the passionate lovemaking she'd just shared with Domenico, the memories bringing a smile to her face at the same time as her toes curled as she anticipated his return and a repeat performance.

It was only slowly, as the time ticked past, that she began to wonder what had happened, and where her ardent lover had got to. And that was when a sneaking feeling of unease crept its way into her soul.

What was taking him so long? What was it about the phone call that had been so important that he had to answer it now—and away from her?

Alice's eyes flew open, all remnants of sleep deserting her in a second as her thoughts went back over the things Domenico had said before he'd left the room.

'Now that you're staying we have all the time in the world.'

*Now that you're staying.*

She hadn't said anything about staying. Hadn't agreed to anything. Knocked off balance by the passion of Domenico's kiss, swamped by the hungry feelings it had awoken in her, she had been thrilled to hear him say that he didn't want her to go. But she hadn't actually agreed to anything. His confident assumption that all was now well and that she was going to fit in with what he wanted suddenly jarred uncomfortably, making her pull herself up on the pillows, thinking back over everything else he'd said.

*I knew I could make you stay.* Alice flinched inside at the memory of the arrogant declaration. Was that the triumphant exclamation of an ardent lover or a man who had just carried out a cold-blooded, deliberate manipulation of the woman in his bed?

*I knew I could make you stay...*

Suddenly desperately afraid to face her uncomfortable thoughts, Alice shifted uneasily against the pillows, trying to find another way of looking at things. But no matter which way she tried to send her thoughts to come up with another explanation, they always came back to the same thing.

*I knew I could make you stay.*

What did that remind her of? It was something that made her mind restless, setting her nerves on edge.

*I'll tell you when you can get up.*

*I'll tell you...*

'Oh, heaven help me!'

The words escaped in a panicked rush and she realised just what the nasty, nagging suspicion at the back of her mind was trying to tell her. She remembered now and it made her feel dreadful—taken for granted—manipulated…

*Used.*

How could she have forgotten the very first day that Domenico had come back into her life after she'd tried to walk away from him? The day that he'd arrived at her cottage and openly declared just why he was there.

'This relationship isn't over, Alice, not until I say so. As long as I want you, you stay—and you only leave when I give you permission to go.'

She'd been such a fool! She'd allowed herself to think—allowed herself to feel—allowed herself to be seduced into believing that Domenico's declaration that he wanted her to stay was because he cared for her. Because he couldn't bear to let her go. But she'd forgotten one important thing.

She'd forgotten how he always had to be in control.

Once before, she'd tried to walk out on Domenico Parrisi when he had not been ready to let her go. He'd come after her and brought her back into line, using exactly the same tactics as he'd just employed on her tonight. He'd cold-bloodedly seduced her back into his bed and into his life. And she had been enough of a blind, besotted fool to let it happen.

'Oh, you idiot! *Idiot!*' she reproved herself, clenching her hand into a fist and slamming it down onto the bed in a rush of impotent rage. 'You let him do it! You let him walk all over you!'

She had been just too weak, too stupid. Totally at the mercy of her feelings for this man, she had let him use and manipulate her into doing exactly as he wanted.

Or had she? There had been that look in his eyes, a note in his voice. There had been *something* there—hadn't there?

Or had she simply been fooling herself? Letting herself believe because it was what she wanted most in all the world? Because her days had been filled with hopes, her nights with dreams, that one day, some day, Domenico might come to feel a little for her.

But that had been when she had thought she was going to become his wife. When she had still been carrying his baby, and Domenico had wanted the child so much that he had been prepared to take her along with it. And now that there was to be no baby, there would be no marriage, no future for her and Domenico in any way.

But of course there had been more to it than that. More that Domenico had wanted out of the arrangement, anyway.

He had made it plain that he still lusted after her—that he still wanted her so much, physically at least. Hadn't he declared that to her face so openly?

*I still want you—more than ever, in fact. And as long as I want you, then this relationship continues. No woman walks out on me—none ever has and none ever will.*

Too upset, too restless to stay still, Alice flung back the bedclothes and flung herself out of the bed. The idea of staying there, just waiting patiently and obediently for her man to return to her, waiting for his attentions, was abhorrent to her. She had to get a grip on herself and make up her mind just what she was going to do.

Going to do?

'Oh, dear heaven!' Alice crammed her knuckles against her mouth in an effort to crush back the cry of pain that was almost like the howl of a wounded animal.

What *could* she do? There was only one course of action left open to her.

She'd told herself that if she was no longer considered as Domenico's bride-to-be then she was going to take her dismissal with dignity. All those weeks before, when she had accepted that the man she loved would never love her back, she had packed her bags and gone. If she had to, she would do that again.

And it looked as if she had to.

She might have been weak this once, might have let him win her over this once. She might have succumbed weakly to soft words and even softer kisses, but if she kept doing that, if she kept on letting him use her in this way, then it would destroy her.

She had accepted that he was never going to marry her now, but to be nothing but a mistress like this, doing his bidding, jumping when he said jump, obeying every command, was more than she could bear. She had to get out of here.

Oh, but it would be so much harder this time. Because the first time she had never known how hard it would be to endure the long, lonely days, the dark, even lonelier nights without a sight of Domenico in her life, without ever hearing his voice.

She had been through all that once, and barely survived. She had had to survive because in the middle of the misery she had discovered that she was pregnant. And because of the baby she had had to keep going. Now she was completely on her own, and she didn't know how she was going to survive.

She had to get out of here. She had to get dressed and ready before Domenico came back. She couldn't face him like this. She had to be clothed—armoured—feeling strong and ready before he came back into the room and she had to confront him with her decision.

If he came back now… If he touched her…

'No!'

Whirling round, she grabbed at her clothes where they lay scattered about the room, fallen on the carpet. She wouldn't let herself think about how they had come to be there, about the wildly passionate moments when Domenico had stripped her—and she had stripped him—and they had left their clothes anywhere they had landed. She had been so hopeful then, so joyful, so optimistic...

So blindly, stupidly, crazily deceived.

She had let him do whatever he had wanted with her and she hadn't even questioned why.

Domenico must have thought that he had her totally in his power; that she was his to do with as he pleased.

And why not? Hadn't she given him every reason to think so?

'Oh, damn it!'

The exclamation escaped her as she grabbed up an abandoned shoe, at the same time spinning round to see if she could find its partner. Her grip on the leather was not secure and the sandal went flying from her hand, landing with a thud on top of a dresser near by.

On top of the dresser was Domenico's laptop, still open, with the screen up and the keyboard exposed.

A keyboard that one edge of her shoe had obviously caught on, briefly pressing a key before it bounced off again and fell back to the floor.

The slim computer had obviously not been

switched off but had been left there, abandoned in standby mode, and Domenico had planned to get back to it well before now. It hummed for a second, buzzed, flickered and then came back to life. The screen lit up and Alice found herself staring at the rows of lettering.

Rows of names and message titles. Domenico had obviously been checking his email messages when he had left the machine switched on.

Alice was just about to turn away and find her shoe again when one of the names caught her eye. A very recent message, it must just have come in in the last hour or so because it lay at the very top of the list, the first thing on the screen. And of course the message subject was in Italian. But it wasn't that that Alice was looking at. Instead, her eyes had focused on the list of names at the left-hand side of the screen, and fixed on one name in particular.

A name that she hadn't heard of for a month or more.

A name that she had thought she would never have to hear of again.

A name that Domenico had *sworn* she would never have to hear of again.

*Pippa Marinelli.*

The woman Domenico had refused to tell her about. The woman he had declared had never been his mistress, but the woman with whom Alice had heard gossip link him so closely in the weeks before she had left him that first time.

As she stood and stared at the screen, and that name, it was as if she was once more back in the ladies' room at one of the most elegant hotels in Milan, where she and Domenico had been attending a reception. Shut in one of the cubicles, Alice had been invisible to the group of women who had come in after she had shut the door. The group of women who had then set themselves to primping and preening in front of the mirror while chattering and gossiping non-stop.

It was when she had caught her own name, and then Domenico's, in the middle of the high-speed rush of Italian that Alice had frozen into total stillness, listening hard.

'And did you see that poor stupid English girl—that Alice Howard—draping herself all over Domenico Parrisi out on the dance floor? She was gazing up into his eyes like a lovesick rabbit—and she doesn't even know she's being taken for a ride. Luisa and I were at a restaurant the other night and we saw him there with someone else—another woman. They were dining together—dining on each other, more like! They had eyes only for each other…Luisa said her name is Pippa Marinelli…'

*Pippa Marinelli.*

Alice closed her eyes sharply against the white-hot stab of pain that seemed to sear right through to her soul.

Domenico had said that Pippa Marinelli was not a danger to their marriage—and she had believed him.

But of course that had been when they were going to get married. Now the engagement was off, the wedding had been cancelled; even her dress had been taken away…

And it seemed that Pippa Marinelli was back in town and back in Domenico's life.

She knew she shouldn't do it, but she really couldn't help herself. She wouldn't have been human if she'd been able to resist the temptation.

Reaching out a hand that shook terribly, Alice clicked on the message and watched it open up onto the screen.

'Dom…'

That was the first pain and one that stabbed straight to her heart.

*Dom.*

The shortened, warm, affectionate form of his name. The name he let so few people use—the name, in fact, that she had believed he let only her use. And it had taken her months of being with him, living with him, loving him, before he had let her use it easily.

And Pippa Marinelli began her email, *'Dom…'*

Alice had to fight a brutal little struggle with herself to clear the tears from her eyes so that she could focus on the screen again and read the rest of the message. She blinked hard, swallowed harder and forced herself to stare at the brief lines before her.

Dom—of course I understand why you want me to be more careful. If Alice has miscarried then, naturally, she will be upset and sensitive to everything at the moment, and you don't want her suspecting anything, or trying to probe into areas you don't want her to know about. But don't

worry—she won't find out anything from me. I do know how to be discreet.
Pippa.

'I do know how to be discreet!'

Shock and pain made Alice's head spin so hard that she had to grab hold of the dresser for support.

He had promised! He had *sworn!*

She felt as if everything she had ever believed, every hope, every dream had been snatched away from her and then thrown aside like so much garbage. She wanted to run—she wanted to cry—she wanted to fold her arms around herself. To keep the pain out and to hold herself together.

But then, just as a moan of savage agony escaped her, she knew another feeling. A sudden rush of a new and very different sort of emotion—a wild, fierce pulse of pure, blinding, exhilarating, liberating rage.

She was *furious!*

How could Domenico treat her like this? How dare he?

But of course he had never thought, never suspected that she would ever find out. He had thought that he was home and dry, safe with his *discreet* other woman—while he kept his poor, blind, *stupid* current mistress dangling on a string.

Well, not any more! Her time of being taken for a fool was well and truly over. She was going to confront Domenico over this—and she was going to make sure he knew exactly how she felt.

Dropping the bundle of clothes to the floor, abandoning the dress as too complicated and fussy to get into in the state of mind she was in, she kicked it out of the way and snatched at the nearest thing to hand—the black towelling robe that lay across a chair near by.

Domenico's robe. And it still bore the scent of his body, bringing her up short with a desperate shudder of miserable memory.

But her anger was still boiling high enough to overcome her momentary cowardice. She needed protective clothing and she needed it fast—and this was the best she was going to get. If she hesitated now, she might have second thoughts and lose this glorious rush of heady fury that would give her the strength to confront him as she needed to.

Steeling herself against the intimate scent that twisted in her nerves, threatening to destroy her, she pushed her arms roughly into the sleeves, pulled the towelling closely round her and yanked hard on the belt to fasten it tightly.

Then, before she could have a chance to think, determined not to let herself think in case she weakened in a panic, she pulled open the bedroom door and set off down the long landing, running down the stairs, silent in her bare feet, looking for Domenico, ready to give him more than a piece of the bitterness and rage that was in her mind.

# CHAPTER THIRTEEN

DOMENICO was getting impatient.

This phone call had been going on for far too long, and it was going nowhere. Or perhaps the truth was that it seemed to be going nowhere because his mind just wasn't on anything that was being said. His thoughts weren't even here in this room but upstairs, where the most beautiful woman in the world was lying in his bed, waiting for him.

'So you see…'

The female voice at the other end of the line launched into yet another explanation but her words didn't seem to make any sense. Instead, they all appeared to blur into one another so that he couldn't make out a single separate syllable, let alone a complete word. All he could think of was the image of Alice.

Beautiful, sensual, sexy Alice as he had left

her lying naked in his bed. Warm and content, her eyes sleepy, her mouth softened and smiling, her gorgeous body still flushed a faint pink in the aftermath of the passion that had brought them together.

A stunning, devastating, unique passion that he had known with no one else—and that he desperately wanted to experience all over again. Already, just remembering, he felt his body go hard and hot and hungry and he fought the impulse to tell Pippa to go to hell, to fling the phone down and...

'Do you understand that?' Pippa Marinelli asked suddenly.

Understand what? What had she said?

'Yes—of course,' he replied firmly, knowing that he had no idea at all what he was agreeing to.

Somewhere in the house a faint sound caught his ears and he tilted his head slightly, listening hard. Was Alice moving?

But he could hear nothing else and so he relaxed back against the desk against which he was leaning and prepared to bring the conversation to a halt.

'Well, it's a disappointment, but it can't be

helped; I do understand that. And I'm grateful to you for what you've done. But I think we'll leave it there— What?'

He broke off, listening, as Pippa spoke again. Then shook his head even though he knew she couldn't see him.

'No, I'm sorry, but I can't do that. I really can't see you this week. In fact—'

He broke off abruptly as another faint sound, a change in the air behind him, brought him spinning round to see the woman who had just pulled the door open and come into the room.

Alice.

A tangle-haired, bare-footed Alice, who was dressed—swamped would be a better description—in his black towelling robe, the soft material wrapped almost twice around her slender frame and the belt pulled tight at her narrow waist.

His first thought was the wild, crazy feeling that the room had suddenly brightened; that it was as if someone had just switched on a brilliant light—no, more that the sun had suddenly come out from behind a cloud and flooded the whole space with warmth and glory. Which was totally ridiculous when he remembered that it was well after nine at night and the sun had already set hours before.

That was when he realised that the brilliance, the warmth, was not a real one, but an outward reflection of the effect that seeing Alice had had on him. And just for a moment he allowed himself to hold on to that feeling, to clasp it to him, to let it into his heart. And to recognise exactly what it meant for him and for his future.

But then she took a step forward into the room and the way she looked, the way she moved created another very different thought—the dangerously sensual one that underneath that wrapped and belted towelling she was naked. He could barely see a glimpse of flesh at the neck or almost all of the way down her legs, but he sensed that she had just got out of bed, grabbed the robe and headed downstairs to find him. And suddenly he knew precisely why, in days long gone, when women had dressed in long dresses, with gloves and hats, with almost every part of them covered up, a flash of ankle would send men into a frenzy of desire. The sight of those long, narrow pink feet planted firmly on the polished wooden floor was having such an erotic effect on him that his mind was heading for meltdown and the temptation to toss the phone aside and reach for her was one he was having to fight hard to overcome.

So instead he looked into her face, into those glorious blue eyes that were no longer sleepy but wide awake and glittering with something distinctly worrying, and his wanton thoughts jolted to an uncomfortable stop. The soft, sexy mouth was no longer smiling sleepily—in fact, it was not smiling at all but was clamped into a set, hard line, and every muscle in her throat and jaw was clenched taut as if to hold back some powerful emotion.

This was not the Alice he had left upstairs, he realised uneasily. Something had happened and it had changed her mood completely.

But first he had to get away from this phone call. 'Pippa...' he said, breaking in on the woman's monologue.

'Pippa!'

It was Alice who spoke, the single word coming swift and low but with such an intonation of deadly fury that it brought Domenico up short, silencing him like a slap in the face.

'Pippa Marinelli!'

And before he could blink, before he could even focus his thoughts, she had marched into the room and snatched the phone from his hand, sending a furious glare right into his face as she did so. Her eyes were even brighter now—but it was the brilliance of anger and rejection he saw, her face white with the control she was fighting to impose on her temper.

'Alice…' he began but she ignored him completely, turning her attention to the phone she held instead.

'Pippa Marinelli?'

He had never heard that tone on Alice's tongue before, even when she'd been furious with him. Never heard the way that each syllable sounded as if it were formed in ice, so that he almost expected to see the frozen letters tumble from her mouth and onto the floor, to lie in slowly melting pools of water.

'This is Alice Howard, Signorina Marinelli. I just wanted to make sure that you heard Domenico right—he *really* can't see you this week. In fact, he really can't see you ever again! If you have any sense of decency at all—which

I very much doubt—you'll stay right away from my fiancé in future. Goodbye.'

As Domenico was still stunned into silence by her action, her icy-voiced outburst, she switched off the phone, gave a small, determined nod of satisfaction.

'There, that's dealt with your little floozy. Now it's time to deal with *you!*'

And, directing that look of ice into his face, she lifted her arm and flung the cellphone straight at him.

Alice couldn't believe that she'd actually gone quite that far. It was only as the phone left her hand that she realised just what she'd done—and the potential results of her unthinking actions. Thrown with all the force of the fury in her soul, the small silver-coloured phone would have done some real damage if it had landed squarely where it was aimed, right in Domenico's smiling face. But luckily some defensive instinct, some sixth sense alerted him, and with reflexes as swift as a cat's, his hand came up, caught it squarely and then dropped it onto the desk beside him with a small clatter.

And all the time his eyes never left her face. And

all the time he kept on smiling. In fact, he looked like a man whose dreams had just come true.

'Why the hell are you smiling like that?' she demanded, thoroughly thrown off balance.

He shouldn't be *smiling*. He should be looking—well, at least he should be looking disconcerted, uneasy—*worried*. After all, she'd just walked in on him on the phone to his other woman—and she'd told that other woman to get out of his life in no uncertain terms.

At the very least he was going to have to do some very careful explaining and soothing. At the worst—and oh, how she hoped for the worst!—he had lost Pippa Marinelli for good. And he was *smiling*.

'Why?' she asked again, even more forcefully, using the violence of her tone to try to push some sense into the stupid, crazy brain of hers that was trying to force her away from the justified fury she was feeling and into a weak-minded appreciation of just how stunning Domenico looked. Standing there with his black hair falling forward over his face, his bronze eyes burning brilliantly, his wickedly sensual mouth curved into that wide, shocking smile, he was having a lethal effect on her senses. His long body was devastatingly attractive even in the simplest of clothes, the white shirt and jeans that she had taken off him only a short time ago...

*No!*

She must not think of what had happened such a short time before. Mustn't remember the final betrayal of that coldly calculated lovemaking. The deliberate seduction that had brought her back under his control, made her do exactly as he wanted and ensured that he would have everything the way he wanted in the future.

Or so he thought.

But if that smile was one of triumph, then she was very definitely going to enjoy disillusioning him on that score.

'Tell me!' she snapped when he just continued to look at her with that damn light in his eye, the wicked smile on his lips. 'Why—why—*why* are you smiling?'

'Isn't it obvious?' Domenico said at last and the lightness of his tone was positively the very last straw.

'No, it isn't!'

'It should be,' he countered. 'After all, what

man wouldn't smile when he heard his woman
claim him as her own with quite that degree of
determination and emphasis?'

'Claim—*his woman?*'

Alice found the words were getting tangled up
in the tightness of her throat. She could hardly
get them past the choking knot that seemed to
have formed there.

'I am *not* your woman! And I did *not* claim
you as mine!'

Domenico dismissed her furious indignation
with a wave of his hand, his casual nonchalance
heaping fuel on the fire of her rage.

'Oh, yes, you did, *carissima*,' he assured her.

And then, when she frowned her disbelief, he
went on, using a voice that she could only assume
was mimicking her own.

'"If you have any sense of decency at all—
which I very much doubt—you'll stay right away
from *my fiancé* in future."'

Had she really sounded as cold and determined
as that? Alice almost winced at hearing her
words reproduced in this way. But then she
realised just what words Domenico had empha-
sised—and just what the deliberate emphasis

had meant. And the powerful effect of the fury that had buoyed her up so much until now suddenly evaporated in a rush, leaving her as limp and deflated as a suddenly pricked balloon.

*My fiancé.*

And if she really had claimed Domenico as hers in quite that deeply possessive way, then it was no wonder he was smiling; no wonder his eyes were alight with satisfaction.

He really must think he had her right where he wanted her.

'I wasn't *claiming* you—I was putting her off!'

'Same thing,' Domenico returned easily.

'No, it's *not* the same thing at all. If you must know I only used that phrase to get rid of her— and the truth is that I came down here to do the same to you.'

If she had actually hit him in the face with the phone, or at least slapped him hard, then the tormenting smile couldn't have vanished any quicker. It faded abruptly and without it his handsome face looked totally different.

'Alice—no!'

'Alice—yes!'

She had to harden her heart to say it, fighting

hard not to be deceived by the loss of all warmth from his features, the way the bronze eyes looked bleak and clouded.

'I came here to say goodbye to you—I just got distracted by Signorina "I can be discreet" Marinelli.'

'You saw the email.'

'I saw the email.'

The fact that he recognised the quote immediately gave another twist to the knife in her already desolated heart. He didn't even try to deny anything. Didn't try to pretend that he didn't know what she was talking about.

'And don't expect me to apologise for prying into your private correspondence—'

'I'm not.'

Domenico took a couple of steps towards her, then stopped as her head came up and she eyed him warily, ready to back away if he came any closer.

'I'm glad you found it. Glad it's all out in the open.'

That was the last thing she had expected and her thoughts reeled a little at the shock of it.

'You're glad?'

Was that high-pitched, brittle-enough-to-break

voice really hers? She sounded right on the edge
of despair—which might be how she was feeling
but was most definitely not how she wanted
Domenico to see her.

'You swore that that woman was not your mistress!'

'She's not.'

'That you weren't sleeping with her.'

'Alicia, *adorata*—I'm not.'

'You said that Pi—that she was no threat…that
I would never have to hear about her again…'

'I meant it. And if you hadn't seen that email
then you never would have heard about her! I
was just paying her off.'

'What?'

Momentarily distracted by that *'adorata'*—
that lying, scheming, calculated *'adorata'*—
Alice couldn't believe what she was hearing.

'You were paying—and that is supposed to
make me feel better?'

Domenico's hands came up in a gesture of exasperation combined with determination to be heard.

'I was doing what you wanted—I was getting
her out of my life, our life, so that—'

Seeing him like this, knowing he believed he

was making things better—that he was winning her round—Alice felt her control break completely.

'Paying her off! Getting her out of…! Dom— she called you *Dom*!'

She could barely get the last word out, huge, racking sobs choking her. And in spite of all her determination, her resolve that this was not going to happen, she found that she couldn't hold back the tears that were now streaming down her cheeks.

'Oh, sweetheart!'

Domenico moved forward so swiftly, his arms coming round her before she had any chance of anticipating it. She tried to fight against his hold, but her struggles were impotent against his strength.

'Alice, *cara*, if that's what's troubling you, I never said she could. In fact, I've asked her time and again to stop using that name—your name— but she is a very stubborn woman and she just wasn't listening.'

'Maybe you didn't insist hard enough.'

Through the whirling confusion in her thoughts, it was all that she could manage.

'Or perhaps you didn't want to drive her away.'

'That's certainly part of it,' Domenico agreed,

so soberly that it shocked Alice rigid. 'I certainly didn't want her to give up on me and the project we had together.'

# CHAPTER FOURTEEN

'PROJECT?'

Alice found she was actually shaking her head in disbelief, her eyes clouded in confusion as she looked up into Domenico's face.

'What project?'

But Domenico didn't answer her immediately. Instead he unfastened his arms from around her body and, with her hand in his, led her to the big, black, leather-covered settee that stood on the far side of the room. Pressing her down onto the soft cushions, he went back to the desk and took something from a drawer, then came and sat beside her, holding a tooled leather wallet out to her.

'What's this?' Alice's tone, like her body, was rigid with suspicion and rejection.

Domenico looked straight into her eyes, his bronze gaze firm and unflinching, disturbingly reassuring when she didn't believe she could be reassured—wasn't even sure if she *wanted* to be reassured.

'Open it.'

Then, when she didn't move, he opened the wallet himself and placed it upright in her lap. But all Alice could do was still to stare into his face, unable to look away, unable to trust the wickedly weak feelings of longing and hope that were creeping into her mind, in spite of her efforts to push them back.

'*Look,*' Domenico said, so insistently that she obeyed him automatically, dropping her gaze to what she held.

And she saw at once just what he wanted her to find.

The small white piece of card was tucked into a side-panel in the wallet. And the name on it caught her eye immediately.

Pippa Marinelli—who else? But it was the next line that snagged her attention and held it.

'Pippa Marinelli—private investigator? Dom—what was she investigating?'

His smile was more of a wry grimace, strangely boyish and disarming, and in his eyes there lurked something she couldn't interpret. In any other man she would have said it was a sort of defensive apprehension—but in Domenico?

'Me,' he said.

'You? But what…?'

Her hand moved, her fingers closing around the card, meaning to pick it up, study it more closely, but Domenico's touch stopped her, held her frozen.

'Wait,' was all he said, and, riveted by the raw note in his voice, she could only sit there in silence and do as he asked.

This time, Domenico reached into a larger section of the wallet and took out a small white envelope. Handling it with care, he opened it and took out the piece of paper it contained, then held it out to Alice.

Her confusion growing with every second, she took it with a care that matched his and stared in bewilderment at the image she held. Printed on cheap paper and in rather garish colours, now rather faded, it was a shabby, worn holy picture of the type that many Catholic Italians put into their prayer books. A picture of a tonsured monk in white robes with a black over-garment that fell almost to the floor, exposing only his bare feet in rough leather sandals.

'Who?'

'St Dominic,' Domenico told her. 'My patron saint.'

'Your…?'

She was reduced to nothing but single syllables, unable to think in any other way.

'Let me explain.'

Domenico didn't touch her, or make any move to try. He didn't need to. There was something so raw and open in his voice, in the bronze burn of those amazing eyes, that she couldn't have looked away if she'd wanted to. He held her effortlessly and mesmerically just by the sheer force of his tone, his absolute stillness.

'I told you that both my parents are dead. It's not the truth—well…'

He caught himself up, sighed deeply then raked both hands through the jet-black sleekness of his hair, ruffling it desperately.

'The truth is, I don't know. I don't know if my parents are alive or dead. I don't even know who my parents are, or were—and neither does anyone else. Even my name is not my own.'

'What?' That brought the startled question from her lips as she struggled to take in just what he was saying.

'I was abandoned as a baby—left on the steps of the church. The church of Santo Domenico in a little town called Parrisi.'

He sat back and watched as Alice absorbed these facts, slowly thinking them through, trying to make them make sense.

'Domenico—Parrisi…'

'That was the name the nuns in the orphanage gave me. Because of where I was found and because of this…'

One long finger touched the shabby little picture that still lay in Alice's open palm, and his eyes were darkly shadowed as he looked down at it.

'This was left with me—it was in the blanket that was wrapped around me. My mother must have put it there because she at least wanted me to be given the name she'd chosen for me. It's the only thing I have of her. The nuns gave it to me when I was five and…'

The way he hesitated, the deliberate pause before he went on and the intent burn of his eyes on her face left Alice in no doubt at all that what he was about to say was the most important thing of all.

'No one—*no one* else has ever seen that or touched it until today.'

'No one…' Alice echoed, beginning to understand the meaning of what he was saying, but unable to believe the significance of what it seemed to mean for her.

'I hired Pippa because someone I knew said that she had had some success in tracking down the parents of adopted children,' Domenico was saying, his voice seeming to come from a long distance away. 'I thought she might be able to help me find my parents, or at least my mother, but I needed someone who could be discreet. For all I knew, I could be the result of a rape, or my mother might just have been little more than a child herself—so I made her swear to keep things quiet.'

'To be discreet,' Alice managed hollowly, going over that revealing email in her mind and now seeing it in a very different light.

There were new tears on her cheeks, tears she had barely been aware of having shed. But this time they were tears *for* Domenico, not tears of pain at something he had done.

'So you see, Pippa was never any threat to you—except in one way.'

The sudden deepening of his tone brought Alice's head up, looking at him through tear-filmed eyes.

'What way?' she managed hoarsely.

'I was afraid that she might turn up something so terrible from my past that I would never be able to ask you to marry me. But then—'

'No, wait a minute!'

Unthinking, Alice lifted her hand and laid it across his mouth, gently stopping his words.

'You—are you saying that you hired Pippa before I left you?'

He had to have done, because already then his name was being linked with the other woman. The lunches he had had with her had been spotted—gossip had started.

'And that was because—because…'

She couldn't continue. Didn't dare to go any further in case it didn't mean what she was beginning to suspect—to hope—that it meant. But Domenico answered her without the slightest hesitation.

'Because I was hoping to ask you to marry me

but I didn't think it was right to do so when I knew nothing about myself—about my background, my parents. What did I have to offer you—?'

'You had the only thing that really mattered— you had yourself.'

Her voice shook as she spoke, the full impact of what he was saying finally hitting home.

The man who had claimed that he didn't do marriage had been planning this all the time. He had brought in a private investigator, let her into secrets he had been carrying with him for all his adult life—and all because he had wanted a chance to propose marriage. And she—Alice— had walked out on him, declaring that she wanted more fun!

The memory made her so restless and uneasy that she couldn't sit there and stay still a moment longer. Releasing the precious picture back into Domenico's hands and getting to her feet, she prowled around the room for a moment, trying to find the strength to speak, and knowing that Domenico was watching her all the time.

'That fun thing…' she muttered at last, turning back to him and looking down into his deep, dark eyes. 'I never meant it. It was what I heard about Pippa and—and—the fact that I didn't think you loved me.'

'I didn't make it easy for you.' Domenico got slowly to his feet, his eyes locked with hers all the time. 'But I didn't want to say anything in case…'

'I know.'

Once more Alice laid a finger across his mouth to silence him. She wanted to kiss him into quietness but she didn't yet dare.

'I understand.'

When he held out his hands to her she took them, feeling their warmth and strength close around her, holding her tight.

'But I couldn't let you go,' Domenico continued. 'So when I came to find you—'

'To find me?' Alice broke in. 'But I sent you a message saying…'

'Saying you needed to talk to me, I know. But I was already coming after you. And then you had my ring on your finger so nothing else mattered.'

'Your ring…'

Once more Alice was blinking away tears, but this time they were not tears of sympathy but ones of real distress.

'I wore your ring, but only because—'

'No!'

It was Domenico's turn to silence her, and this time he did it with a kiss. A kiss that was so strong and tender and so—so *loving* that it took Alice's breath away, destroying all her words with it.

'No, *cara, no*! Never. It wasn't just because of the baby—though I tried to tell myself that was the only reason at the time. I wanted you in my life, I couldn't live without you, and when I thought that you were going to have my child— a family of my own at last—I felt as if I'd been given the world.'

'The world—a family—but I lost…I failed…'

Now the tears would not be held back. They tumbled down her cheeks, thick and fast, but Domenico gently wiped them away and kissed the places where they had been.

'Oh, no, beloved, never think that. I would have wanted that child, would have loved him or her so much, but you are my family—you are my world. If I have you in my life then it will be enough.'

His kiss was long and slow and it spoke of promises, of futures—of happiness. But there was still one thing nagging at Alice's thoughts.

'But—the wedding. When I came back from

the hospital, you'd got rid of everything—even my dress. I thought that was because you didn't want to think about marriage any more—that you…'

'That I wouldn't want to marry you because you were no longer pregnant with my child?' Domenico put in when she hesitated, his voice as deep and burningly sincere as the passion in his eyes. 'You couldn't be more wrong, my love. I had everything cleared away because I didn't want to pressure you. Because I wanted you to know that you were free—free to make whatever decision you wanted, without being tied to a promise you had made under duress. I wanted to give you time and space to recover from the miscarriage and then I was going to ask you to marry me all over again—and this time I was going to do it properly. I wanted to marry you even more than before because I'd had a taste of what it could be like to have a wife, a child—to be a…a family.'

If Alice had had any doubts before then there were none in her mind now. To see a man as strong and sure as Domenico always appeared suddenly stumbling over his words, to catch the glint of sheening tears behind the fringe of thick dark lashes shielding his bronze eyes, was something that struck straight to her heart with its message of love and need and the loneliness of loss.

And now at last she dared to move forward, sliding her arms around him and pressing close, lifting her face, taking his mouth in the kiss she had been yearning to give for so long—for a lifetime, it seemed.

And Domenico responded ardently, taking all that she was offering, and giving it back a hundredfold. Giving her his love, his devotion, all his heart in that one kiss.

Alice could have stayed like that forever. Either that, or she would have wanted to take Domenico back upstairs to bed, to give herself to him in the truth of love and the knowledge that he felt the same. But Domenico was strangely resistant to her gentle urging, her attempts to edge him towards the door.

'*Momento, cara,*' he said softly. 'Wait—there is something I must do…'

And as Alice stared in astonishment he suddenly dropped down onto one knee and caught hold of her hand, pressing a lingering, loving kiss on the back of it.

'Alice—my love—I want to do this properly this

time. I want you to know, to be in no doubt that I adore you, that without you my world is empty…'

Disbelievingly she saw him pull something from his pocket and recognised it as the engagement ring that she had flung at him in a fury earlier that evening. He must have gone back to the living room and hunted for it, keeping it with just this moment in mind.

'Beloved Alice—my life, my heart are yours. Will you marry me and be my wife, my family, for the rest of my life?'

Reacting purely instinctively, Alice knelt too, coming down on the carpet beside him, deep blue eyes locking with the longing, loving gaze of this man she loved so deeply.

'I'd be honoured to do so,' she told him with deep-voiced fervour, every last trace of uncertainty or tremor gone from her voice. 'Oh, yes, yes, my darling. Yes, I'll marry you.'

In the same hospital where just fifteen months before he had kept a long, lonely vigil at Alice's bedside, Domenico once again sat beside her sleeping form, but this time in a totally different frame of mind.

This time he couldn't wait for her to wake, couldn't wait to see her smile and know that her happiness was mirrored in his own face.

Even as he thought it Alice stirred, murmured sleepily, opened her eyes and looked around.

'Dom?' she asked softly. 'Was it real? Or did I dream?'

'No dream, my love,' he hastened to assure her. 'It's perfectly, wonderfully real. Our son was born last night and he's as perfect, as healthy and strong as any baby should be.'

'Our son,' Alice echoed happily, her joy glowing in the deep blue eyes. 'Can I hold him?'

'Of course.'

Crossing to the bassinet that stood on the other side of the bed, Domenico gently lifted his tiny, twelve-hour-old son from the mattress and handed him carefully to his mother, watching as she cuddled him close, dropping a soft kiss on the little upturned nose.

'How can I ever thank you for this gift?' he said, coming to sit beside Alice on the bed, putting one arm round her and with the other helping her support their child.

Alice looked up into the intent, loving gaze of the

man who was her husband, the father of her child, and her heart clenched in love and understanding.

When Domenico had been no older than her newborn son, his mother had wrapped him in a scruffy blanket, put the picture of St Dominic in the bundle with him, and abandoned him on the stone steps leading up to a village church. She could only be thankful that a much happier fate awaited her already beloved baby son.

'You don't need to thank me,' she told Domenico softly. 'Just promise to love me—and this little treasure—for the rest of your life.'

'I promise,' Domenico told her, and as his mouth took hers in a long, deeply passionate kiss she knew that it was a promise he had every intention of keeping.

# MILLS & BOON® PUBLISH EIGHT LARGE PRINT TITLES A MONTH. THESE ARE THE EIGHT TITLES FOR AUGUST 2006

---

## THE BILLIONAIRE BOSS'S FORBIDDEN MISTRESS
Miranda Lee

## MILLION-DOLLAR LOVE-CHILD
Sarah Morgan

## THE ITALIAN'S FORCED BRIDE
Kate Walker

## THE GREEK'S BRIDAL PURCHASE
Susan Stephens

## MEANT-TO-BE MARRIAGE
Rebecca Winters

## THE FIVE-YEAR BABY SECRET
Liz Fielding

## BLUE MOON BRIDE
Renee Roszel

## MILLIONAIRE DAD: WIFE NEEDED
Natasha Oakley

MILLS & BOON®

Live the emotion

0706 Ron

# MILLS & BOON® PUBLISH EIGHT LARGE PRINT TITLES A MONTH. THESE ARE THE EIGHT TITLES FOR SEPTEMBER 2006

———————— ❧ ————————

## THE GREEK'S CHOSEN WIFE
Lynne Graham

## JACK RIORDAN'S BABY
Anne Mather

## THE SHEIKH'S DISOBEDIENT BRIDE
Jane Porter

## WIFE AGAINST HER WILL
Sara Craven

## THE CATTLE BARON'S BRIDE
Margaret Way

## THE CINDERELLA FACTOR
Sophie Weston

## CLAIMING HIS FAMILY
Barbara Hannay

## WIFE AND MOTHER WANTED
Nicola Marsh

MILLS & BOON®

Live the emotion

0806 Rom LP